Vlad V (Book 3)

Vampire Slayers

By Mit Sandru

Chivileri Publishing

Copyright © 2014 by Dumitru Sandru

ISBN-13: 978-1-942612-03-2

This is a fictional story. All names, persons, organizations, businesses, places, and occurrences are fictitious and spring from the imagination of the author. Any resemblances to actual people or events are completely coincidental.

Table of Contents

The previous book in this series is *"R.I.P., The Death of an Honest Vampire"*

The US intelligence agencies have a massive database, including pictures that can identify any person in the US and abroad. A search has found a photograph of Vlad V Draculesti, a man living in present-day Manhattan, dating from 1851. How can that be? Why does Vlad look the same in the 21st century as he did in the 19th? Who is this man who has lived such a long life? Homeland Security Federal Agent John Miller discovers that Vlad V Draculesti is a vampire, and he blackmails Vlad for billions of dollars, threatening to divulge that information to the authorities or to the evil Dr. Hellinherr, who is trying to create a super-race of people through the use of vampire blood. But Vlad V, because of a mishap, is now dying of old age, and all he wants is to die in peace. Cat Sanders, his great-granddaughter, and his three vampire friends—François, Angelique, and Mundibuto—come to his rescue. They foil the intelligence agencies' plans to discover the real identity of Vlad V Draculesti, and they eliminate the corrupt federal agent's threat. Never underestimate a vampire, his cunning great-granddaughter and his vampire friends.

Chapter 1. The Confession

I've done terrible things in my life.

I am a good woman and a good Catholic, or so I thought, until recent events in my life caused me to wonder who I have become.

One day, out of the blue, I found out that I'm related to a vampire, Vlad V Draculesti. He was my long-lost great-grandfather. I should say, he was my great-great-great- . . . great-grandfather, because he was 560 years old when he died of old age a few weeks ago. It sounds ridiculous to say that a vampire—the undead, who should live forever—would actually die from old age, but that's what happened. He had an unfortunate and peculiar accident that caused his aging and his death as an old man. He was the nephew of Vlad the Third, also known as Vlad the Impaler, or Dracula. My great-grandfather was Vlad the Fifth, and he was a good man—and a vampire.

I am his descendant, but I'm not a vampire. My last name is not Draculesti; it is Sanders, and I go by the nickname, Cal. Vlad was thrilled to have found me, and I was glad as well, since my parents are dead and I have no other relatives. Unfortunately, Vlad died a couple of months after I met him, and now I'm alone again. I've inherited his entire fortune and I'm a multibillionaire, with more than one hundred billion dollars in assets. Life should be good: I am 23 years old, blonde, attractive, intelligent, educated, and street-smart, too.

Contrary to common belief, vampires do exist and they live among us. Yes, they suck human blood and live long natural lives. They get their life energy from human blood, but they don't need to drink a lot of it. Nor do they kill their victims. And no, they are not burned by the sunlight—they can live happily in the daytime, although they prefer the night. They don't sleep in a coffin or on a bed of dirt, but in a nice firm bed. Their food is not blood but alcohol—vampires can drink like fish without getting drunk. And if one bites you . . . sorry, but you won't turn into a vampire, even if you drink their blue blood. Yes, vampire blood is blue. To become a vampire, you must inject the blue blood into your bloodstream, and then you'll transform into a vampire.

Vlad V and many of his vampire friends were against turning humans into vampires. They considered themselves human mutations. They tried not to contaminate the world with their blue blood and took extreme measures to prevent infection among humans. But Vlad was dying, and what do you do with a dead vampire? Any doctor would have determined that a dead vampire was not one of us. And the dead vampire would have ended up in labs, private or military. Vampires are stronger and faster than any human will ever be. They heal fast and don't die easily. Imagine a nation with an army of vampires. It would become the ultimate power on Earth. For another country to develop its own vampire army, it would take only one drop of blue blood. Soon after that, instead of a nuclear weapons race, there would be a vampire army race. And that would be the end of humanity.

Any human would be a drop of blue blood away from becoming a vampire.

It was part of the effort to destroy Vlad's body after he died that started the unhappy chain of events. It should have been a simple task. After Vlad died, we took his body to a military-grade biohazard incinerator, which Vlad owned, and cremated his body. Except that US Homeland Security had become suspicious of Vlad's longevity and, together with the NSA, they began investigating Vlad, who could not die peacefully with the US intelligence agencies after him. Three of Vlad's vampire friends came to his aid. They were Mundibuto, possibly the only black vampire in the world, an American but living in Africa now; Angelique Brazeau, a sexy, voluptuous redhead from France; and François Le Beau, a drop-dead stunningly handsome Frenchman. God, is he gorgeous! Anyway, I came up with the brilliant idea of using another man's dead body to fake Vlad's death and stop Homeland Security and the NSA from snooping around.

It would have worked, too, if it weren't for a corrupt federal agent, Tom Brenner, working for Homeland Security under the alias John Miller. Brenner had his own agenda with Vlad V Draculesti. He discovered that Vlad was a vampire, and while investigating him for Homeland Security, he tried to blackmail him. But Tom Brenner was greedy, and he wanted even more. He contacted a certain Dr. Hellinherr, an old nemesis of Vlad's. Brenner partnered with Dr. Hellinherr to capture

Vlad and use his vampire blood to create a super-race of human-vampires.

To ensure the successful blackmailing and abduction of Vlad for Dr. Hellinherr's experiments, Tom Brenner had his illegitimate daughter—Veronica Seyler, who I knew—lure me out of my apartment so that Brenner's accomplices could kidnap me. Raping and killing me would have guaranteed to eliminate any witnesses to their crime. Fortunately for me, François, Vlad's vampire friend, rescued me and killed the kidnappers. Angelique and Mundibuto abducted Tom Brenner, and soon after, he departed to the world beyond—or the one below. Veronica Seyler was the only one who survived and knew about the plot. The FBI and the New York City police were searching for her, to shed some light on Tom Brenner's disappearance. But she went into hiding.

Homeland Security closed the case against Vlad V Draculesti after he died. That was after his fake death, which I orchestrated. Soon after that, though, Vlad died for real, and we cremated his remains. Vlad had asked me to spread his ashes in Transylvania, from the clock tower in Sighisoara, a last wish that I promised him I would fulfill.

Oh, one more thing: I have a drop of blue vampire blood from Vlad. It is in a diamond amulet inserted behind my right ear. I don't want to become a vampire, but if I do, all I need to do is squeeze the spot behind my ear, and the vampire blood will infect me. Then there would be no way back, and I would become a true vampire. But that's only in case I want to become one.

My heart and my soul are troubled, and confession is the cure for the burdened soul. So I went to confession at the Church of St. Vincent Ferrer, near my home in Manhattan.

"Bless me, Father, for I have sinned." I knelt in the confessional booth, feeling the urge to open up about what I had experienced and to come clean about the criminal acts I had willingly masterminded and participated in over the past few weeks.

"How long has it been, my child, since your last confession?"

"Six months, Father." I came to the conclusion that I'm not such a good Catholic, but I hoped this confession might improve my status with God or at least make me feel less guilty.

"Hmm. And what are your sins, my daughter?"

What were my sins? Let's see. I've kept the company of vampires. Telling the priest that would make him think that I was fraternizing with the undead. He would probably get out of the confessional booth, grab me by the ear, and would either throw me out of the church or take me to the crypt and perform an exorcism on me.

"Well, it's hard to say." I searched for a more mundane sin to tell the priest.

"Take your time, my child."

No, I couldn't confess about the vampires. I could tell him that I masterminded the fake death of a vampire, Vlad Draculesti. No, no vampire confession. Maybe I should tell him how I participated in the killing and cremation of a man, a corrupt federal agent, so I could present his ashes as proof of Vlad's death. Would the priest consider this a confession to a crime? Would he call the police? For sure he had a cellphone on him with 911 on the speed dial. Oh, well—no killing and cremation confessions, either.

"Well?" The priest pressed softly.

I needed to confess something. I thought hard.

"I took a man to my bedroom and had intercourse with him out of wedlock." I felt relieved that I could say that much. A burden lifted from my soul.

After confession, I didn't leave the church immediately. I sat in a pew and prayed. I miss my great-grandfather and think about him often. Sure, he sucked blood just like all vampires do, but toward the end of his life he relied on blood banks. He had lost his canine teeth and couldn't bite anymore.

I lit a candle and prayed for Vlad's soul—he said he had a soul—and I also prayed for a successful trip to Transylvania.

On my way out of the church, I noticed a young man in Goth attire sitting in a pew at the back. He looked relaxed, with his arms spread out over the back of the bench as if he were a tourist admiring the church's architecture. Maybe he was a Catholic Goth?

Chapter 2. Watchers

Back at home—Vlad's Fifth Avenue apartment was mine now—I sat at Vlad's desk, thinking about the trip to Transylvania. I wondered how long I would continue to refer to everything as Vlad's. Even dead vampires don't take anything with them into the world beyond, wherever that may be. Vlad assured me that there is no hell, unless you create one. As a vampire, as one of the undead, hell was the logical place for him to go. But the real vampires are not the undead, just another form of living humans. Vlad believed in God and thought that he would go to heaven. I will verify that when I see him again after I pass away. I shuddered to think of my own death.

I looked at the painting of Elena, my maternal great-great-great- . . . great-grandmother and Vlad's wife when he was human. How beautiful and radiant she was! I look just like her, but perhaps I'm not as beautiful as she was. I hope Vlad is reunited with her in heaven. Elena and Vlad V had a daughter, Anina, and my blood lineage descends from her.

I was alone. My vampire friends had departed. Angelique left for Rio de Janeiro, François for Montreal, and Mundibuto for Africa, no country specified. Homeland Security didn't follow me anymore, although I was sure the NSA, with its big ears, listened in on me all the time.

Outside my window, the sky was gray, and it was raining off and on. Across Fifth Avenue, in the park, a dark figure caught my eye. It was the Goth dude from the church; he was watching the entrance to my building. Because he never looked up, I wasn't sure if he knew where I was, on which floor I lived. There was no chance he'd get to my door with the doorman and the security guard in the lobby. Was he an agent of Homeland Security? No, he was too noticeable. Federal agents blend in and are inconspicuous until you notice their suits. He wasn't an agent. I wondered what he wanted.

I took a pair of binoculars from the desk and focused on the Goth fellow. Black pants, black boots, studded black leather jacket, black eyeliner and black painted nails. Oh yes, and a dog-collar choker with spikes on the outside. A serious agent of the dark. Who could he be? And what did he want? I pondered that. Goths either worship vampires or are vampire slayers. Maybe he somehow found out that Vlad V Draculesti was a vampire and that I was related to him? Was he hoping to find Vlad, the vampire? Maybe I was paranoid and the Goth fellow wasn't after me.

There was an easy way to find out. I went down to the street. The guy was across the avenue, leaning against a tree in the park, cool as ice. I opened my umbrella and walked in his direction. I didn't make eye contact with him; I wanted to give him the impression that I was just walking by. He didn't make eye contact with me, either, looking away in a detached manner.

When I was in front of him, I stopped. "Hello there. What's your name?"

He looked caught off-guard, but he recovered quickly. Being cool was mandatory for the people of the night. He didn't respond, but he looked me straight in the eye, as if daring me.

I dared him. "OK, Spike. What do you want?"

He said nothing but continued staring at me, perhaps wishing it were night so he could jump me.

"Are you a wannabe vampire slayer?"

His eyes narrowed. Good sign. He confirmed what I suspected.

I turned around to leave but then I added, "Be careful what you wish for. Dying violently is not pretty or fun." I walked back to my apartment, unconcerned about my threat.

From the window I checked to see if he had kept his post. He was gone. Hopefully, they were going to leave me alone. But then I saw another Goth figure across the avenue. She was a tiny gal. Hmm. There was more than one of them, and they were watching my building in earnest. Or looking for Vlad, who was no longer among us.

Chapter 3. P.I.

Well, well, well. Those people are insane if they think that somehow they've scared me. Sure, I went outside and confronted Spike without a bodyguard, but it was in broad daylight. Once night fell and I was alone, I should be easy to snatch. Or so they might think. If they only knew what formidable paranormal protection I have—my Strigoi, my ghostly guardians. I inherited the Strigoi from Vlad, and the first night I met him he used them against two would-be robbers. The robbers were lucky to have survived.

I thought for a moment. They know I've noticed them. Did they expect that I would panic, be afraid? Call Vlad to scare them away? And if Vlad appeared, would they jump him? If Vlad were alive and had met them, those people would be hanging from the tallest branches of the park's trees.

If they weren't after Vlad and just wanted to get a reaction from me, as if I were a scared chick, what would I do? Call downstairs and ask security to call the police to shoo them away? Call my lawyers to get a restraining order against them? Yes, those were possibilities. But the watchers stayed at a reasonable distance, hanging around in a public park. They hadn't done anything illegal. Yet.

I called downstairs.

"Hello, Miss Cat, this is Mario," the doorman answered before I could say anything.

"Mario, have you noticed young people, dressed in black, keeping watch on our building's entrance?"

"Yes, I have, Miss. Would you like me to call the police?"

"That would be great. Thanks, Mario!"

It didn't take long before an NYPD blue and white patrol car stopped at the opposite curb. Two beefy cops stepped out of their police car and approached the tiny Goth girl. She was so puny and the cops were so massive, it made me feel sorry for her.

They talked. Actually, the cops talked to her, and she didn't say anything, just stared at them. Tiny pulled out her cellphone and called someone, after which she walked away.

Well, that was easy.

But maybe not. A bit later, another young Goth man took a position at the same place where Tiny stood. They were persistent. By now the cops had left. The lobby phone rang. "Miss Cat, this is Mario. Another person in dark clothes is watching now. Should I call the police again?"

"No, thanks, Mario. Let him get wet."

They'd gotten my attention, if that's what they wanted. I searched through Vlad's list of contacts, and I found two private investigation agencies that Vlad had on retainer. I called the first one. "Mallon PI Agency. How may I help you?"

"This is Cat Sanders. I am the great-granddaughter of the late Vlad Draculesti."

"Yes, ma'am. I'm terribly sorry for your loss. Mr. Draculesti was a great man. I'm Robert Mallon. Please call me Rob. What can I do for you?"

"Please call me Cat, Rob. I see that my great-grandfather had you on retainer."

"Yes, ma'am—I mean, Cat. What would you like to do?"

"I would like some PI services from you and to continue with the retainer."

"That would be great. Thank you very much," Rob Mallon said with relief in his voice, probably because I wasn't canceling the retainer and was keeping him employed.

"And I need your services right away."

"Absolutely. What would you like me to do?"

"How soon can you get to my apartment?"

"Twenty minutes—I'm in Midtown."

I gave him further instructions, and I waited for his call when he was across the avenue in Central Park.

I descended into the lobby to put my plans into action. Mario looked at me with concern. "Don't worry, Mario," I told him. I didn't want him to call the police.

Outside, it had stopped raining, and the late afternoon sun was breaking through the clouds. I sniffed the wet air, which enhanced the trees' fragrance and the exhaust fumes from the passing cars. I turned right and walked on the avenue, as if I were taking a stroll. The Goth man who was watching me was tall and lanky. I nicknamed him Lanky, and he followed me on a parallel path on the opposite side of the street. Bob Mallon—who I now knew from the pictures he had sent me—was nowhere in sight. He was either a good PI or he wasn't around. I preferred and hoped he was a good PI.

At the corner, I turned onto the side street and walked away from Central Park. I walked briskly, checking in a small mirror to see if Lanky was following me. He cut across the avenue, through the traffic, and was pursuing me. The street was desolate and shady, and there was not a soul in sight. A plan always seems better in your mind, but reality is different. Here I was, a blonde young woman, in shorts and a tank top, walking on an empty street, albeit during daylight hours, and some galoot was following me. Darn, I should have worn sneakers in case I needed to run.

As I picked up the pace, I checked my mirror again and saw Rob the PI behind Lanky. I was relieved to see him. Although I was confident that my Strigoi would protect me, the fear of being followed never left me. At Madison, I turned right and then right again onto the next street until I reached my building's entrance on Fifth Avenue. I'd given Lanky a walk around the block to make sure it was me they wanted.

My cellphone rang. "Cat, are you OK?" Rob the PI asked.

"Thanks, yes, I am. Did you get a good look at him?"

"Yes, and I took several pictures. I don't think he ever wanted to approach you, just shadow you, like a stalker."

"That's what I figured, especially when I confronted Spike earlier today."

"You gave them nicknames? What do you call the tall one?"

"Lanky. I'm not sure when he will be relieved of his watch, but I'd like to know where he's coming from."

"No problem. Did you notice which direction they come from or go to?"

"They go south."

"Good. I'll let you know as soon as I find something."

At sunset, Lanky's replacements arrived, and he took off, going south on Fifth. Two Goths replaced him, a middle-aged woman who walked like a goose and a guy with a Mohawk down the middle of his shaved head. Two more new characters. I called these two Goose and Mohawk. They stood about one hundred feet apart, leaning on whichever tree was more comfortable, and they watched.

Chapter 4. The Silver Coffin

Rob called me at around nine in the evening. "Cat, I followed Lanky to a nightclub."

"What's its name?"

"The Silver Coffin. It's a Goth nightclub. Lanky went inside and never came out." Rob paused for a second. "He either is spending the night inside, or he left through another exit."

"Thanks. A Goth nightclub makes sense."

"I can't go inside in my current attire—they wouldn't let me in. They have two Goth bouncers at the door."

"Is it open?"

"Yes, but I figure the crowd will arrive after midnight."

"Thanks, Rob. That will do for right now. Let me know if I need to add more money to the retainer account."

The Silver Coffin—the name of the club didn't ring a bell. A Goth nightclub, vampire slayers, Vlad being a real vampire—it all added up, but how would they, those Goths, even know about Vlad being a vampire? There were only two people who suspected Vlad of being a vampire: Tom Brenner and Dr. Hellinherr. The Goths didn't seem to be connected to Dr. Hellinherr. Tom Brenner was dead . . . of course— Veronica Seyler, his daughter, knew about Vlad. One way to unravel this mystery was to visit this Silver Coffin nightclub. I checked my wardrobe and found plenty of black clothes, including stiletto-heeled black boots. I even had a black wig and a silver studded belt. Let's go see what this place is all about.

At midnight, I was all decked out as a Goth girl. Although I'm fair-skinned, I applied a lighter shade of make-up so my face became luminescent white. I clipped some gaudy earrings on and put on all the silver rings I have on my fingers.

The trick was to evade the watchers outside my apartment. That was not going to be hard, since I wouldn't leave through the front door, but through one of the safe-house apartments. Vlad had built two adjacent apartment buildings, and he—and now I—owned two apartments at the same floor level with the Fifth Avenue apartment, in case he needed to exit without being noticed or to evade capture. I left through the Green Apartment, on the north side, which had a different lobby on the adjacent street.

I took a cab on Madison to the Silver Coffin near East Houston in Goth Town. The cabbie didn't know where the nightclub was and I gave him directions. I guess Goths don't often use cabs. We arrived at our destination; I paid the fare after I assured the cabbie that I'd be OK by myself at night in that neighborhood. It was nice of him to be concerned, but once I was out of the taxi he took off in a hurry.

The Silver Coffin was a dump. The entrance was on a backstreet. I expected flashy neon signs and stuff, but there were none. It had a small silver sign, not even lit, with the club's name on it. The only thing that would make you think this place was a club was a short line of Goths waiting near the velvet ropes at the entrance. Two Goth bouncers guarded the front door, as Rob had described. I popped some chewing gum into my mouth and acted cool and sullen. I had a lot of black mascara on, and my lips were pale, just like my skin. No signs of fear on my face, I strolled confidently to the front door, from where the two Goth bouncers were eyeing me.

"Name, please?" Frankenstein's twin asked me.

I looked at him, unblinking. But he was not persuaded by my billionaire-Goth stare. He pointed to the end of the line. I got on line.

This was such a new experience for me. I worked and went to school full-time, so I didn't get to sample much of life, and never the Goth life. No one waiting on line smiled or joked or conveyed any expression of any kind. They spoke very little. Goth was cool but sad. I was getting the hang of the style's behavior quickly.

Not everyone entering the club had to wait on line like the rest of us Goth commoners. There were VIPs arriving in stretch limousines, and other Goths with reservations were allowed in without waiting. It was a half hour past midnight, and more Goths were lined up behind me. The line moved quickly and Frankenstein's lookalike pointed to my small black purse. I opened it for him to see my make-up kit. Darn, I forgot to put my switchblade in my right boot. He waved me in, I dropped a Jackson for the entrance fee, and I was ushered inside through black velvet curtains.

I stepped into total darkness and almost tripped when I missed a few steps going down. Walking in stiletto boots in the dark down the stairs requires Goth skills, and I was still in training. I touched the wall and let my eyes adjust to the very low light. It took me a moment until I could see anything. Most of the lighting inside was black light, giving everything an eerie feeling of Halloween, except the pumpkins were missing. If they had psychedelic posters on the walls, I might think that I was transported back to the hippie era. But this was Goth, all black and somber. And it smelled like pot.

Goth rock music pumped out of the speakers. A few slow-moving couples, illuminated by dim black lights, occupied the dance floor. No one was using either one of the two dance poles. Pity. There were tables around the dance floor and some people were sitting down, but more Goths stood or leaned against the walls like mannequins. The bar had a bit more light but only for the bartender's benefit. A red neon sign, *The Silver Coffin*, hung over the bar. I supposed it was red neon to symbolize blood.

Everyone had a drink of some sort in his or her hand. To blend in, I went to the bar and ordered a Merlot, a Goth-appropriate red wine. They had liquor, too, but beer prevailed. Guinness and German beers were the standard. Who would have thought Goths and good beer go together?

Ten bucks for a glass of Merlot. At least it had a skull around the glass's stem. I leaned against a wall and took a sip. What crap was I drinking? It tasted like wine from a box. I'd sure become snooty since I'd indulged in Vlad's—now my—wine cellar.

As my eyes continued to adjust I could see more. Farther away, in niches in the wall, there were booths, some with closed black curtains, some with open curtains, but they were completely dark inside. If there were people inside, I didn't want to know what they were doing in there and didn't have to guess. A half-naked woman rolled out of a dark booth but quickly crawled back in, mooning the rest of the establishment. No one gave a hoot.

Chapter 5. Vampire's Lair

The inside of the nightclub was large, and I noticed two stairways leading upstairs. My recon mission ongoing, I took the stairs to the upper level. It led to a room similar to the one below except it had an oval opening right over the dance floor below. There were two iron cages, suspended from the ceiling by chains, over the opening. Two Goth girls were in the cages. One was dancing, while the other one was splayed out on the floor of the cage, seemingly moribund, with her legs and arms protruding through the bars and hanging over the edge of the cage. I wondered how they climbed inside or what they did for bathroom breaks.

Heavy chains with shackles hung from the simulated stonewall, but no Goth was shackled in them yet. The night was young. Coffins with hinged lids were propped up against the walls. Standing up, of course. The coffins were double-sized to accommodate couples. How original! At least one of them was rocking, so I didn't bother knocking. The lid on another coffin opened, and two Goth men came out. They slapped each other's butts, satisfied with their coffin experience. They were good-looking, too. I sighed—what a waste of manhood!

Drugs were being sold discreetly, and it seemed as if just about everyone had taken something either to stay awake or to act like a zombie. I walked around, acting inconspicuously, or at least not raising the suspicion that I might be a narc. I wondered if they had security cameras anywhere in there. Possibly not. It was too dark. I descended on the other set of stairs to the level below.

To my surprise, on the ground level to my right, I discovered a new entrance, rather hidden, with stairs going down and a bouncer standing guard there. I ignored him and nonchalantly approached the stairs. He stepped in front of me and crossed his arms to block my advance. "This is the VIP lounge, Miss. Access allowed only by invitation."

Needless to say I didn't have an invitation, but I was curious to see what was down there, so I said, "I'm a friend of Veronica's." I wondered what reaction I'd get using the name of my old nemesis.

Although it was dark, I could see that he had an earpiece and an attached mic. He said, "Friend of Veronica's." I wasn't sure if he was talking to me or into the tiny mic on the side of his mouth. I waited, taking a sip of my red wine and acting as if I belonged.

Shortly, a man came up from downstairs and extended his hand to me. "My name is Cadogan. Who are you?" The thirty-something man was of medium height and dressed in Goth attire. In addition to many piercings, he had two stainless steel horns on his forehead. The reflection from the black lights made his bleached blue eyes look even more sinister—the contact lenses did a good job on his eyes in the dark.

"What's up? I'm Angelique." I shook his hand, deciding not to give him my real name.

Cadogan studied me intently, his eyes lingering over my breasts. "Angelique. I don't believe I've met you before. Unfortunately, Veronica is not here tonight. Would you like to come down below into the Vampire's Lair?"

"Sure." Without waiting for him, I walked toward the stairs. He caught up with me quickly and offered me his arm. A Goth gentleman.

"Where did you meet Veronica?" Cadogan asked me as we descended.

Where the hell should I say that I met her? Tattoo or piercing parlor? I had no piercings and no visible tattoos on me. I'd have to buy some fake tattoos and deck myself out with them and more metal if I needed to come back here. "We're pals from long ago. Do you work here?"

"Yeah, kind of," Cadogan said with a slight smirk.

We arrived down below. This lower level was definitely not fire-department approved. There was where the serious business of the dark was conducted. Down here the music was not as loud and or as fast as upstairs; it was more like electronica, heavy metal, and Gregorian chants combined into one. Red velvet armchairs, sofas, and golden low tables in Louis XVI style furnished the room. The whole place was decorated like a medieval chamber, and some walls were covered in black or burgundy drapes. Candles and several gas torches lit the place. In the middle of the room, on a pedestal surrounded by four candelabras, was placed a silver coffin. Dracula's, I presumed. The coffin was not a rectangular shape like modern ones, but wide at the chest and tapering toward the head and the feet. There were no flowers on it, and the chamber didn't give the impression of a mortuary wake. But it created the right atmosphere in this room, a freakish catacomb. The coffin gave it a nice touch.

"How's your drink? Can I get you a glass of blood?" Cadogan offered.

Did he say blood? "Human?" I asked.

"I can offer you goat blood on the house. Human blood costs $100 per glass."

"I'll stick with my wine. Is this Dracula's chamber?"

"Homage to the great vampire. The Vampire's Lair." He spread his arms with admiration.

"Did you ever meet him?"

Cadogan looked at me intently, as if to discern whether I was making fun of him or if I was serious. "I haven't had the privilege of meeting and being bitten by him."

"Do you want to become a vampire?" I played along with the tale that, once bitten, you became a vampire.

"That is my life's desire," he sighed.

"I thought that Goths were vampire slayers."

"Depends on who the vampire is," replied Cadogan.

"I see no homage to Princess Eleonore von Schwarzenberg in this room." I had learned her name from Vlad's file. She was a vampire from the 17th century, sucking blood from her victims somewhere in Austria.

"Who?" Cadogan was ignorant of other vampires.

"If you want to become a vampire, you should know about all the other vampires." I gave him an amused sideways glance.

"Well, I'm just a soldier in the Order of Dracula. I'm sure Princesses Melantha and Philomena know about them."

"Princesses? Who's the king?"

"There is only one. King Vlad Dracula, of course."

"Last I heard he was a count and he was dead."

Chapter 6. Melantha and Philomena

"Of course he's dead." A tall woman with long black hair in a long black evening gown said insolently.

"I mean dead dead. Haven't you read the obituary in *The New York Times*?" I said.

"Who are you?" she demanded.

"Pardon me, Princess Melantha, this is Angelique, a friend of Veronica's," Cadogan introduced me.

"Is she now?" She came closer. "Angelique. I never heard your name spoken by Veronica."

"We knew each other in the past. We're trying to get reacquainted again."

"Is that so?" She scrutinized me. "Why don't we sit down, and you can tell me more." She indicated the red velvet chairs and a sofa surrounding a golden table.

Well, we might as well palaver. I was sure that she and the other princess, whatever her name was, were aware of what went on in the past between Veronica and Cat. She and I sat down, while Cadogan stood by her chair with his arms crossed.

Princess Melantha snapped her fingers. "Hey, Pink-Ass. Fetch me a glass of human blood." Quickly, a feeble young man arrived, holding a silver tray with a crystal glass filled with blood. She addressed Cadogan, "Invite Princess Philomena to join us." She snapped her fingers again. "Pink-Ass. Fetch a glass of human blood for Princess Philomena."

I watched, half-amused, the action unraveling within this "royal court." Princess Melantha was far from being a vampire or royalty. She was a mere human with a dark imagination.

"Why do you call that fellow Pink-Ass?"

"Because his ass turns pink when I spank him."

I didn't press for more details.

Cadogan opened one of the varnished wood-plank doors with black iron hinges and another woman, dressed in a similar long black evening gown, joined us. She was Melantha's twin, except her black hair was combed sideways and her locks fell over her left breast.

"Princess Philomena, my dear. We have a special guest here . . ." Melantha paused, not remembering my name.

"Angelique." Cadogan came to her rescue.

"Yes, Angelique." Melantha was not pleased by Cadogan's help. "Angelique says she's a friend of Veronica's."

"And she says that King Vlad Dracula is dead dead," added Cadogan. He received a very annoyed look from Melantha.

"Angelique. Pleasure. I am Princess Philomena." She extended her hand, which I shook.

What was with all this formal etiquette, as if we were at Buckingham Palace? I smiled, but just with my mouth. "Pleasure's all mine. I didn't know that I would be meeting royalty."

"Royalty at our king's court. Commoners outside this establishment would not understand," said Princess Philomena, rather piqued by my comment.

Commoners like myself. I got that. She was maneuvering to impress and humble me. I hid my amusement under a calm face.

"What was all that about King Vlad being dead dead?"

"Well, it was in *The New York Times* obituary column."

Philomena and Melantha exchanged quick, puzzled looks.

"Myself, I found out from Veronica about the obituary. She knew Vlad personally."

"Who is this Vlad you're referring to?" Melantha asked eagerly.

"Vlad the Fifth Draculesti. He was a real vampire—Veronica told me."

"And how could this vampire Vlad the Fifth die, if he were not dead already?"

"Old age." I shrugged.

Philomena and Melantha exploded with laughter, joined by Cadogan. Even Pink-Ass chuckled, as he offered a similar glass of blood on a silver tray to Philomena. The two clinked their glasses and took sips of blood.

"That was a good joke—a vampire dying of old age," said Philomena. "And Veronica told you that? When was the last time you talked to her?"

"By phone, a month or so ago. I had lost track of her and she found me, and we talked and she told me that she hangs around the Silver Coffin, and to come and find her here. Do you know where she is?" I displayed my best innocent, inquiring face.

"She's not here tonight. But I'm sure she will be here tomorrow evening," said Philomena.

"Cadogan, would you get Angelique's number, please?"

My phone number? I had an untraced phone on me, the same one I called Veronica from when I was kidnapped by her father's goons. "What's your number, Cadogan? I'll call you from mine and you'll have it." He told me his number and I called him. Now he had my number and I had his, if I needed it.

"Bloody good," said Melantha. "Do you live in the city?"

"Brooklyn."

So now that I've found out that Veronica was there, which was good and bad news, it was time to exit. They were getting too inquisitive. I was not sure they would allow me to leave without finding out everything there was to know about my real intentions and identity. Time for plan B.

"I haven't seen Veronica in ages. She was the most beautiful girl in high school, with big green eyes, natural blond hair, and long legs. I wonder if she reconciled with her rich family." I described someone unlike Veronica to throw them off.

"Green eyes and a natural blonde? Rich family?" questioned Melantha. "What's her last name?"

"Miller," I said, smiling. I had to smile, because I gave them a name that either they knew or they didn't. If they didn't, I was looking for the wrong Veronica and should be able to exit gracefully. If they knew about Miller, Brenner's alias, I may have to do a quick dance to get out of here.

"Dear, I think we have a misunderstanding," said Philomena. "You may be searching for the wrong Veronica in our midst."

"This is the Silver Coffin, right?"

She nodded. "The Silver Coffin Nightclub."

I covered my mouth with my hand, feigning embarrassment. "Maybe she said Silver Coffee Inn? I don't think she mentioned 'nightclub'." I stood up. "I'm so mortified. I came to the wrong place. I'm so sorry. Please forgive me for my bungling." Faking total humiliation, I ran to the exit, climbed the stairs, walk-ran across the dance floor where the Goths were dirty-dancing, climbed a few more steps, passed between the bouncers at the door, and I was out on the street.

Lucky for me, a taxi had just unloaded some passengers and was available. I climbed in and told the cabbie to take me to Grand Central. He took off, and I sighed with relief. But behind me, from an underground garage, a motorcycle roared out and followed the cab.

Chapter 7. The Getaway

Being followed wasn't good. They were not happy with my intrusion and wanted to know who I really was. How could I shake off my pursuer? I could lose him in Grand Central. Nope—I had stiletto-heel boots on. What else? I could bribe the cabbie to drive faster and shake him off.

I read the cabbie's name on the ID tag. "Abbas, I'll give you one thousand dollars if you drive faster and lose the motorcycle following us."

The black-bearded Abbas glanced in the rearview mirror nervously, first at me, then at the motorcycle. "Trouble with boyfriend?"

"Something like that. One thousand dollars. Let's see how good you are." At 2 am there was hardly any traffic in Manhattan. It should have been easy to step on the gas.

"No, no, Miss. Don't want lose license and job. Feed many kids at home."

"Two thousand dollars."

"No, no. Many kids at home."

"Five thousand."

"No, no want."

"How much do you want?"

"Nothing. Want no trouble. We go to Grand Central."

Bummer. This bribe thing worked only in the movies. I had to get rid of the biker. "Take me to the first entrance on 42nd Street." I checked his meter, and I didn't want to argue with him about the fare. I pulled a Benjamin from under the double bottom of my purse. "This is for the cab fare. Keep the change." Abbas took the bill and smiled. He had many mouths to feed.

As we got closer to Grand Central, I pulled my boots off. The first entrance on 42nd Street was in sight and I shouted, "Stop there at that entrance, and fast!" The Benjamin improved his understanding of English, and he burned rubber as he stopped hard at the entrance.

I jumped out and ran inside, but quickly turned to the right and stood flat against the wall. My pursuer busted through the doors and removed his helmet, searching for me. He was a she—a Goth she. She was beefy enough to be mistaken for a guy. A group of people were exiting, and I moved along with them outside. My taxi was still there at the curb. I opened the door and got in, staying low in the back seat. "Drive, and I'll give you another hundred."

Abbas almost jumped out of his seat—the crazy woman in black was back. He gulped as if he were about to say something, but he didn't argue and drove away without turning his meter on. Good man. The biker must have realized what had happened, because I heard her bike approach the taxi at high speed. I sank to the floor. Good thing I had black clothes on. "Drive normally," I told Abbas.

The biker caught up with us, slowed down, and peered into the cab on the passenger side. She slowed further, pulled in behind the cab and checked the driver's side. Unhappy with the results, she pulled up to Abbas's window and rapped on it. Abbas rolled down the window and I heard the biker ask, "Did you see which way the woman in your cab went?"

"Inside. Don't know." Abbas's voice was high-pitched and fearful.

"Fuck you!" she shouted and took off on Madison, back toward Grand Central.

I raised my head carefully. "Go down on Fifth and then make a right-hand turn on the first street." I put my boots back on—what a stroke of luck to have caught the same cab! He turned right on 39th. "Turn right on Avenue of the Americas." I gave him two Benjamins. Now he could feed his brother's kids, too. "Stop here on the right side."

I got out and bolted into the nearby subway station. But I didn't have a MetroCard, and I needed to move fast. A young woman was about to swipe her card to get in. "Miss, I'll give you twenty bucks if you swipe the card for me as well." She agreed and I was inside.

Any train would do, but the F train going uptown was just coming in. Two stations later, I exited at 57th Street. A few more blocks north on Fifth from here, and I was going to be home. I walked out of the subway at the corner of 6th Avenue and 57th Street, and I stopped dead in my tracks. The biker, dressed in black leather, was waiting for me at the curb. She looked at me through her dark visor. I shuddered.

Avenue of the Americas and 57th Street were deserted at this hour of the early morning. I was alone with her. How did she follow me here and what did she want? She and I stared at each other, she on her bike and I in my high heels.

They probably placed a radio transmitter on me at the nightclub. There was no time to search for it now. I couldn't outrun her in the street. I couldn't outrun her in the subway station—at this late hour, the trains ran infrequently or not at all. I looked to the left. I looked to the right. I saw no way of escaping.

Chapter 8. The Call

"Remove your helmet!" I demanded as I approached her.

She stood there and stared at me through the dark visor, while the bike was idling.

"What do you want?" I asked.

The biker lifted the visor. It was a man, not the she-Goth, and I didn't recognize him.

"I'm sorry I scared you, but I'm waiting for my girlfriend." He pointed to the subway exit.

I sighed with relief. "Oh, I see. Have a good night then." I swung my purse over my shoulder and walked toward Central Park. I looked back after a while and a woman came out of the subway exit and climbed onto the back of his bike. They passed by me just as I was about to turn on 59th toward Fifth Avenue. He even waved to me as a farewell.

I leaned against a wall, trying to make sense of this night and my close call. But what if they did put a bug on me? I checked my clothes, especially on my back, but I felt nothing. Maybe it was just my imagination. Better get back home, and fast.

Although I was not far from home, I stopped a cab and took it to my Fifth Avenue apartment. With my black wig in hand, I got out of the cab as Cat. The doorman took a moment to recognize me in my black attire, but he called the elevator for me and saluted me as I entered.

I lay in my bed, unable to sleep. What were those people up to? Veronica was behind this, unless they played along, but I didn't see why they would do

45

that. I was rather gutsy to go there and claim to search for Veronica. I improvised well, taking the name of Angelique. For sure she wouldn't mind, while she was having fun in Rio. And I was lucky to get away from the biker, the one from the nightclub. I laughed out loud, remembering the other biker outside the subway station and fearing the worst. I may have ghostly bodyguards, but they haven't appeared yet. On the other hand, no physical harm has been done to me so far either, so they haven't needed to defend me.

This was crazy. I was supposed to go to Transylvania to spread Vlad's ashes, not look for trouble in a nightclub. I wondered if the Goth-Dracula-Order minions would follow me to Transylvania. They were sure deep into Dracula and vampire beliefs. What's their game plan? Money, Dracula, or me?

I finally managed to wake up late the next morning. My breakfast served as my lunch as well. Outside, the Goth watchers were there, keeping an eye on the entrance. I recognized Spike and Tiny, paired now to make me worry even more. I was not worried, but I was still curious about their intentions.

As I was preparing my brunch, the noon news was on TV. On the screen, they showed a yellow cab crashed halfway through a boutique window. I raised the volume to hear better what had happened. Something was unsettling about the news.

The news reporter appeared on the screen in front of the wreck from across the street. "This accident happened in the early morning hours. The driver's name was Abbas Moghadam, and he was pronounced dead at the scene. The police attribute the accident to a drive-by shooting, disclosing that he was shot in the head prior to the crash. He was not robbed, as they found the cab fares, including several hundred-dollar bills on him. The police are asking for any witnesses to contact them in case they can provide additional information about this murder."

Jesus! Abbas, my cabbie from last night, was shot and killed? Who could have done that? The biker who followed me? Why would she kill him? That didn't make sense. I wanted to believe that Abbas's murder wasn't related to the biker from the nightclub. But if it was, then there was some serious crapola going down at the Silver Coffin. I shook my head in disbelief. But why wonder? Wasn't Veronica involved with Brenner, her father, who kidnapped me and eventually would have had me killed? Yes. But what did the cabbie have to do with all this? They're sending me a message, maybe.

I lost my appetite. This was more serious than I originally thought. I looked out my window, and my watchers were there, keeping vigil.

My cellphone rang. I jumped.

Cadogan's name appeared on the phone screen.

"Hey, Cadogan."

"Hey, Angelique. Just checking to make sure you got home safely earlier today."

"Thanks, Cadogan. Everything is OK. Sorry for the intrusion last night."

"No problem. I was asked to call you and tell you that Princess Philomena will get in touch with you shortly."

"Really! You have to announce her call?"

"Well, she wants to talk to you, not leave a voice message," Cadogan said.

"She'd better hurry up, because I'm about to get in the shower."

"Stand by please."

"Wait! Why would she call me?"

Cadogan hung up without answering. The suspense mounted. Should I wait for her call, or do whatever I please?

My phone rang.

"Hello," I answered.

"Hello, Angelique, darling. This is Princess Philomena."

"Princess Philomena?" I acted surprised by her royal call.

"It is I, darling. I hope you had enough sleep."

"Yes, I did. What can I do for you?"

"Is your name Angelique or Cat?" Her voice had an edge now.

Oh well, they've found out who I was—so much for that secret. "Does it matter?"

"It does. You see, Veronica does not know of any Angelique. But she identified you as Cat Sanders, the billionaire, of Fifth Avenue."

Huh—Philomena pronounced my full name and emphasized that I'm a billionaire. Was that on purpose or a slip of the tongue? "I see. Veronica remembered that I'm a billionaire. Good. Where is she?"

"You can meet her at the nightclub," Philomena replied in an oily voice.

"Is it money you want?"

"Money? Who mentioned anything about money, darling?" She chuckled.

"Do you know she was involved in my kidnapping? I could let the police know where to find her."

"And if they find and arrest her? She could tell them that your associates killed three men and her father. She has a voice recording of a conversation between her father and a certain Dracula. Your name is on that recording, too." Philomena paused to let her words sink in. "Besides the recording, Veronica has all the information her dad, Tom Brenner, had. And Dracula really exists, and he killed four people."

Chapter 9. Threats

I played dumb. "Whatever you've said makes no sense. I don't know what you're talking about."

"That's what I expected you to say, darling." Philomena snickered. "You are implicated up to your earlobes in murder. You would be lucky not to get the death penalty, but for sure you'd spend the rest of your life in prison. What good would all those billions do you then?"

It was time to break this discussion thread. "Why did you kill the cabbie last night?"

"I didn't kill any cabbie."

"If not you, then the biker who followed me."

"What biker? Did she come out of the club? No."

Most people would assume a pursuing biker would be a "he," but Philomena said "she." "How do you know the biker was a woman?"

"Look, this has nothing to do with the subject we're discussing. Who gives a fuck about a dead towelhead cabbie? Don't try my patience." Her voice turned steely.

"Or what?"

"This discussion isn't over yet. Get ready for repercussions if you don't cooperate with our forthcoming proposal."

"I'll take my chances with the NYPD. Veronica, on the other hand, . . . tell her I wish her luck." I disconnected the call.

What did they have on me? Nothing. They may have something on Vlad, but Vlad was dead. If Veronica says that she asked me to go barhopping the night of my kidnapping, I'd admit to the invitation, but I'd say I didn't make it out the door because I felt indisposed and changed my mind. I'd say I was safe and snug in my apartment all night long.

Nevertheless, I wanted Veronica, now that she's resurfaced. This loose end would bother me forever. I needed to tie it up. It was time to get Rob Mallon, the PI, involved again. I called him and invited him over.

Rob Mallon was a stocky, balding man with an affable smile. From what I'd read about him, he was a retired cop turned PI. He didn't look like an ex-cop, but that was his allure as a PI: friendly and nonthreatening.

"Come in, Rob." I invited him in and we walked to the parlor.

"Hello, Cat. I want to tell you again how sorry I am about Mr. Draculesti's death."

"Thank you. I appreciate it." I gestured for him to sit down. "But life goes on and brings new and different challenges every day. By the way, can I offer you something to drink?"

"I'm fine, thank you. Yes, life is complicated. It keeps me busy, though." He had such a comforting smile that it put me at ease. He took a moment and admired the expensive artwork and oil paintings on the walls. "What would you like me to do? If you'd like, I could propose some alternatives to get rid of them." He nodded his head toward the window.

"Thanks, but right now I would like you to document their presence, and find out who they are and where they live. I've even given them nicknames, as I mentioned before." I had him follow me to the window. "That guy is Spike, and the gal is Tiny."

Rob took a compact camera from his pocket. He extended the telescopic lens and took pictures of the two. "The pictures are dated and time-stamped," he assured me. "Do you want to use these pictures against them?"

"I might. Right now, I want to know who they are and where they live."

"What if they are planning on harming you?"

"They would not be able to get to me while I'm here."

Rob gave me a doubtful look. "You may need round-the-clock bodyguards."

"I've had a bad experience with bodyguards. Anyway, yesterday when I ventured outside they were just stalking me. Now, I think they may want to kidnap me."

"That's serious. We need to get the police involved."

"It is just extortion."

"Blackmail? Care to tell me more about it?"

We returned to the parlor. There was no need to make him privy to my kidnapping affair. That stuff had to be kept secret for now. But I could tell him about Veronica's suspicion about Dracula. "As you know, my great-grandfather's name was Vlad Draculesti, as in Vlad Dracula."

Rob turned serious. "The vampire?"

"Yes. Of course, it is nonsense, since he died and I cremated his remains. He was an old man, just like any other old man. However, the people from the

Silver Coffin believe that my great-grandfather is Dracula and that he is still alive."

"Why do you suspect that?"

"I was there last night."

"At the Silver Coffin?"

"It is open to the public. I went in for a drink and some recon."

"You're gutsy, I'll give you that."

"Most Goth people are pretty benign, just living a dark fantasy, and that's what the nightclub provides them. However, I met two women there, Princesses Melantha and Philomena—"

Rob straightened up in surprise. He pulled out a small notebook and scribbled their names in it.

"They're princesses at the court of the Order of Dracula. I also met a fellow there, a foot soldier, by the name of Cadogan."

"How did you manage to talk to them?" Rob asked.

"There's a certain woman, her name is Veronica Seyler. In the past she was interested, shall we say, in extorting money from Vlad on suspicion of him being a vampire. I went to the Silver Coffin last night—actually, it was midnight—and asked for Veronica on a hunch. The princesses came to talk to me and acknowledged that Veronica would be there. They also wanted to know how I knew her and who I was. I gave them my cellphone number to let me know when Veronica would be in the nightclub." I showed Rob my phone.

"You shouldn't have done that," Rob said.

"Well, it was a tight situation there for a moment, but I wanted to hear from them. I managed to get out on the excuse that I was looking for the wrong Veronica after all."

"So they didn't stop you or attempt to abduct you?"

"No, I managed to get out." I omitted telling him about the cab, the biker, the chase, and the cabbie being shot later on, probably by the same female biker. I told him just what he needed to know for the current assignment. "Philomena called me earlier. She talked to Veronica, and she recognized me as Cat."

"But didn't you tell them you were Cat?"

"No, I used the name Angelique."

"Ahh, I see. Veronica didn't know an Angelique, but, probably from the videos they took of you at the club, she recognized you as Cat."

"Probably."

"What did Philomena want?"

"She danced around the money issue. She didn't want to talk about that on the phone, but that's what she wanted. I told her to take a walk."

Rob scratched his chin, trying to wrap his head around my story. "This is serious stuff. We need to contact the police."

Chapter 10. Something Is Amiss

"No, not the police, not yet. I want to know more about them first. Be careful, though. These people are not strangers to bloodletting."

"You mean murder?"

I nodded.

"How do you know that?"

"In a lower section of the nightclub, they offer and drink human blood."

"They're freaks, but that doesn't mean they've killed anyone."

"It's just a hunch, but I think this is more than a club. It is a cult that worships the dark."

"In that case, it will be difficult to penetrate their inner circle."

"I don't want you to get in. No offense, but I don't think you'd pass as a Goth, no matter how hard you try."

"I can send other associates in there."

"I just want to know who they are and where they live. For now."

"You're right. But don't you try to mess with these people. They could be venomous snakes."

"Thanks, Rob. I can handle them for right now."

"OK. But promise me you'll let me know if this escalates."

I nodded several times.

"In that case, I'll have to hire several associates to do a round-the-clock surveillance."

"That's fine. How much do you want me to transfer into the retainer?"

"Fifty thousand will do for right now."

"OK. One more thing: How can I get the blueprints of the building where the Silver Coffin is?"

"I'll get them for you."

Rob went to work and kept me posted by text message, and he sent me pictures of the watchers as well. Their numbers expanded, as they watched now only in pairs. Rob gave the new ones nicknames as well.

I printed the pictures and posted them on a board in my office. I set up a spreadsheet and kept track of their watch hours. The hours were random, and it was obvious that many of them did not have full-time jobs, if any jobs at all.

The next day, Rob sent me a blueprint and pictures of the building, which occupied an entire block. It was a massive red-brick building of ten stories, with arched windows on the top floor. The street level was three stories high and had many shops in it. The floors above were either offices or apartments.

The Silver Coffin entrance, as I personally found out, was located on a narrow one-way street. According to the blueprints, the Silver Coffin occupied the length of that entire backstreet, and it had three levels, one underground, as I recalled from my recon visit. Under the nightclub there was a large basement, designated as a storeroom, which was no such thing. The Vampire's Lair was in there. And as I remembered, it was much smaller than the footprint of the actual basement. That so-called basement had many other secret chambers. What was going on down there?

The rest of the building's underground, not the portion under the Silver Coffin, was a three-level parking garage. That meant they could have built secret exits to the garage. Knowing how Vlad built his safe-house apartments, I was not surprised anymore by the lengths people would go to when they didn't want to be found or caught by the police.

My phone rang. "Hello, Rob," I answered.

"Hello, Cat. After three days of monitoring them, we've found that there is something very peculiar going on at the Silver Coffin."

"Yes?"

"All the watchers identified so far return to the Silver Coffin but never come out through the front door."

"There are several emergency exits, even from the nightclub's second level onto the fire escape," I said, looking at the blueprints.

"I've had people monitoring all possible exits, but none of them exited from anywhere in that building. They must have secret exits."

"From looking at the blueprints and what I remember from visiting that place, they could have exits into the parking garage, or even up into the apartments above."

"There are residential apartments on the backside of the building, above the nightclub. The entrance to the apartments doesn't have a doorman, only video surveillance and a squawk box. There is no way to get in without being identified first."

"Did you take pictures of the people coming in and out of that place?"

"Yes. I'll send you their pictures. Most of them are Goths, but not all."

"What if all of them are Goths, but the non-Goths are cleaned up for their day jobs?"

"Could be. This place is something else. Cat, have you told me all you know about this nightclub?"

"Rob, I didn't know this place existed until I visited it. The place is a mystery to me, too, and it may be more than a nightclub. Let me see if I recognize any of the people you saw going in and out of the apartments."

"OK, I'll just monitor them. God knows what we've stumbled on!"

"Just check who they are and what they do."

"OK. By the way, I had to hire more people to help out than I originally envisioned. Could you deposit another $50K?"

"No problem, Rob. Are you using off-duty cops?"

"Yes. Why?"

"Just like you smell something foul there, so will they. I wouldn't want the police opening an investigation until I can get to the bottom of this."

Rob paused. "Are you sure you're not with some intelligence or law enforcement agency doing some black ops investigation?"

"You're a good PI, Rob. But what you see is who I am. I'm no secret-agent woman."

Chapter 11. Speculations

Rob sent me pictures of some of the residents in the apartments above the Silver Coffin. I had no problem recognizing Melantha and Philomena, both in Goth get-ups and in plain clothes. They were not twins; they just looked alike. I identified Cadogan in Goth makeup, but without the horns, and maybe Pink-Ass. And some of the watchers, but not all of them. Well, at least the main players lived in the apartments above the nightclub—how convenient. Many of the watchers I identified from my window never exited the Silver Coffin or through the apartment entrance. What exits did the other watchers take when they came to take their posts in the park?

I paced around the office, thinking, occasionally checking the current watchers outside my building. There were, in total, 27 individuals keeping watch on me. I remember Cadogan telling me that he was just a soldier in the Order of Dracula. He never kept watch, though. They had quite an army. How did they move so stealthily?

A light bulb went on in my head. I got on the computer and checked the location of the building on Google Maps. What do you know! The building was just two blocks away from the 2nd Avenue subway station . . . the F line station . . . the same F line that stops at the Avenue of Americas and 57th Street station . . . the same F line that I took when I returned from the Silver Coffin. That could be just a coincidence. However, could they have built an underground access to the subway station for their clandestine moves? More than likely.

I got on the phone. "Rob, this is Cat. I think I know where the watchers are coming from."

"From where?"

"From the 2nd Avenue subway station, two blocks away from the building. They must have an underground access to that station, and from there they take the F train to Central Park."

"How did you figure that out?"

"I checked on Google. I think all of them live in the apartments above the nightclub."

"Wait a second—that's the same train station they exit when they return to the Silver Coffin, which they enter through the front door but then depart from underground. I'll post watch in the subway station and see if they take the train from there."

"It looks that way. By the way, I identified Melantha, Philomena, and Cadogan, and even a waiter going by the name of Pink-Ass. The others I didn't recognize, but I'm sure they are all involved in the plot at hand or other endeavors. I'm cataloging all the people you took photos of and the ones keeping watch."

"Are you sure you're not a secret-agent woman?"

"Not a chance."

Whatever this cult was doing had nothing to do with me until recently, when Veronica must have put them onto me. She probably contacted them and made them a business proposition to extort money from me. But what will be their next move?

I could video them from my window and call the police. This thing could unravel when restraining orders are issued against them. But then, what would they do afterward? Kidnap me? Maybe. But why haven't they done that already? Maybe they suspect I have bodyguards. Or they're afraid of suffering the same fate as my previous kidnappers. Little do they know that I don't have my vampire friends with me any longer.

The other thing was, what if I were to panic and leave? Maybe they are counting on me to stick around. Why? Because I, or Vlad and I, want to get back at Veronica? They must know that she is the only witness to what happened in the past. Maybe they believe that Vlad or I are after her to silence her, and that eventually we'd come to them, to the nightclub . . .

My untraced phone rang and I answered it.

"Hello, Cat."

I recognized her voice. "Hello, Veronica."

Finally, she was calling me. Hmm. She's got guts. Instead of running and hiding, she continues her quest to get money from me. I'm worth billions, and a few good Goth wannabe-vampire slayers would serve her well for the task of extortion. At least that could be her thinking. Philomena told me that she had proof that vampires exist from a recorded conversation between Tom Brenner and Vlad.

Chapter 12. Veronica

"How are you doing, girl?" she asked me, as if nothing horrific had ever happened to me because of her.

"Veronica, you must be out of your mind. I don't know if I should feel sorry for you or hate you."

"Why would you feel sorry for me?"

"Because you continue to jeopardize your freedom, perhaps your life."

"How sweet! I bet all rich bitches feel that way. Well, I hate you, and I'm not going to give up until I get my pound of flesh. Let's see how you feel then!"

"And how are you going to do that? I have money to buy all the protection I want, while you're being sought by the police. Why don't you come clean?"

"Ha, ha, ha! I am clean, you bimbo—"

"If you disrespect me, I will hang up."

"Yeah, you're right. Let's be polite. You inherited billions, and Vlad killed my father. How polite can I be?" she shouted.

"Let's make something clear: I inherited money from Vlad because he was my great-grandfather. You have no claim to it. Vlad is dead. Period. And your father—if he really is your father—is a criminal."

"He was my father, and you killed him."

"I killed him? Is he dead? I didn't know that." I played ignorant.

"Yes he's dead, and Vlad and his friends killed him."

"I cannot even imagine that being true. Besides, weren't you the one who lured me out to be kidnapped?"

"Luring you out to be kidnapped! That's your word against mine. And it is irrelevant, compared to murdering my father and three others."

"Prove it."

"I have proof of what Vlad said before my father was killed. I have all the documentation and audio recordings about the planning and the kidnapping. And I have proof that Vlad is a vampire and that he's alive."

"What proof do you have that Vlad was a vampire?"

"Testimony from Vlad's girlfriend, Nancy. Does that ring a bell?"

"And where is this Nancy now?"

"You know she's dead. Coincidence? I think not."

"You say Vlad was a vampire because a dead woman said so. Who would believe that BS?" This statement was for the other ears listening in to our conversation.

"Vlad is a vampire and he's alive."

"Be that as it may, you are trying to extort money from me—blackmail me—with some fabricated nonsense."

"I have the recording of the last discussion between my father and Vlad. Dracula."

"Recording? What recording? I've never heard of any such thing." Vlad had thought that if there were such a recording it would be meaningless.

"Would you like me to play it for you?"

"Go ahead."

Veronica clicked on a device, and first I heard some static, followed by:

"OK, Dracula, I know you're here. Come on out," said a man, presumably Miller-Brenner, the corrupt agent. *"In case you want to do something foolish, we've got Cat, stashed in a safe location."*

"What?" It was Vlad's voice, and he was alarmed.

"That's right. Insurance and extra motivation for you to do as I tell you," said Miller Brenner.

"You're not in this by yourself?" Vlad asked.

"No, of course not. I have accomplices." I heard Brenner laughing. *"Don't be foolish, Dracula. You have only one chance to save Cat, and you have an hour to transfer the amount I demanded. I'll text you the account numbers shortly."*

I heard a click.

"What do you think, Cat?"

"I heard a man trying to extort money from somebody named Dracula, who is not my great-grandfather. Besides, you just incriminated your dad of blackmail and kidnapping."

"That's what it seems like. But you haven't heard the best of it. Listen to the amplified recording at the beginning and end of the conversation." Veronica clicked it on again and I heard the following:

"Angelique and Mundibuto, get ready to strip him naked, in case he's wired, and bag him. I'll talk to him, but I'll stay in the shadows." It was Vlad speaking. Another click and then I heard Vlad say, *"Get him!"*

67

That didn't sound good. I'd never heard any of the conversation Veronica played for me, but this last part was when Vlad gave the order to Angelique and Mundibuto to abduct Brenner. That's incriminating evidence against Vlad, if they can prove that it was Vlad.

"I have no idea what you're trying to prove with that nonsense recording." I talked as if I were not at all disturbed by it.

"Are you dense? Didn't you hear your great-grandfather giving orders to Angelique and Mundibuto to get my father? To 'bag him'?"

"My great-grandfather is dead. If he was who you say he was, take it to the police."

"Your great-grandfather is alive and well *and* is a vampire. By the way, who are Angelique and Mundibuto?"

"Never heard of them."

"Why did you call yourself Angelique when you came to the Silver Coffin the other night?"

"It's just another name."

"Are they vampires, too?"

"Vampires don't exist. Veronica, go take a hike."

"You wish! Until I find out the truth and get my fair share to keep my mouth shut, we'll be your shadow."

Chapter 13. Angelique

I disconnected the call. What a bitch! All this watching outside the entrance was to intimidate me into thinking that they know a secret about me for which I need to buy their silence. They might have something against Vlad, but Vlad was dead. That chapter was closed. I called Rob and terminated the monitoring of the Silver Coffin. I considered the watchers and Veronica a nuisance, not a threat.

I'd wasted enough time with this fake intimidation. It was time for me to concentrate on going to Transylvania. I couldn't think of any reason why I should travel incognito, therefore I didn't need a fake passport. If Homeland Security were to follow me, they would be sorely disappointed. I was not going to meet Vlad but to spread his ashes in Sighisoara. If that didn't discourage them and make them leave me alone, I didn't know what it would take.

The travel reservation should not be made from my Fifth Avenue apartment's computer, as the NSA could trace it. Instead, I was going to do that from one of the two safe houses. As I said, long ago Vlad had constructed two adjacent apartment buildings, next to the Fifth Avenue main residence, each connected by secret doors to the main apartment. As far as anyone was concerned, those two apartments, with exits on two different streets, were owned by anonymous people of no specific importance. Now they were mine as well, although the titles were held under aliases.

There was a South apartment, decorated in a color-coded maroon red, and a North apartment, color-coded forest green. Through one of the secret doors, I entered the maroon, or South, apartment, which was fully equipped, computers included. All my travel plans had to be made from there.

As I headed toward one of the bedrooms, which served as an office, I heard something in one of the other bedrooms. Fear gripped me. These apartments were supposed to be empty, with no guests at this time. Angelique, who's used that bedroom in the past, had left for Rio. Who could be in there? I approached the door quietly, heart pounding, wondering what I should do. I was unarmed, and if I found an intruder, then what? It was tough to be alone in situations like this—but wait! In case of danger, I had my Strigoi, my ghostly creatures, to defend me. Cat, you're such a little girl!

Determined that I was going to kick butt, I opened the door to the bedroom and found Angelique the vampire in bed, naked as usual. I jumped in surprise. She jumped in happiness at seeing me. And then both of us jumped into each other's arms.

"Angelique, what are you doing here?" I was so glad to see her. She must have come in through the secret elevator.

"Trouble in paradise, Cat," she said in a tired and sad voice.

"What trouble?"

"I was almost apprehended in Rio. They know I am a vampire."

"Who knows that?"

"SNI, the Brazilian intelligence agency."

"Oh, my God. But how?"

Angelique shook her head, as if she herself couldn't believe what happened. "Let me put something on, and I'll tell you all about it over a drink."

That bedroom had some of her clothes in the dresser. She didn't seem to have any luggage or clothes, except for a blue jumpsuit that was discarded on the floor. From one of the drawers she pulled out a green silk gown and slipped it on. I remembered that gown from when I had first met her. Actually, she was naked then, too, and Vlad asked her to put some clothes on for my sake.

In the parlor, Angelique poured herself a tall glass of bourbon and sat next to me on the sofa. "What can I tell you? Vlad was right. They can identify just about anyone nowadays, and they definitely know who I am. Have you spoken to François or Mundibuto?"

"Only to François. They looked for him, too, but he got away. I haven't heard from Mundibuto. By the way, what happened to you in Rio?"

"After I returned there, I settled back into my Rio nightlife. I could say that things were normal, although, in retrospect, I should have paid attention to the distance-finder beams from surveillance cameras all around that have increased in number. I was being surveyed and photographed, but I wasn't on the alert. About a week ago, after a fun night out visiting a few nightclubs, I returned home about 4 am and went to sleep.

"They were waiting for me, and at sunrise they moved in to capture me. A helicopter hovering outside my apartment window blasted out my windows and dark shades. They figured that, if I were a vampire, the daylight might fry me. Fat chance! My front door was kicked in, and a dozen or more of the SNI's Special Forces rushed in. The noise of the helicopter and the bright light of the rising sun woke me up just before they kicked the door down. Unlike Vlad, I don't have a safe house, but I have weapons and, most important, teargas and smoke bombs.

"I detonated as many as I could find. It stopped the agents just long enough for them to put their gasmasks on, but that was long enough for me to break the wall and get into the apartment next door. The smoke was so thick that they didn't realize I was next door already. From the other apartment, which was empty—a little bit of luck there—I opened the front door a crack, but the hallway was full of agents and I couldn't get out that way. The only way out was to descend on the outside of the building from the fifteenth floor."

I gasped.

"Don't worry. Vampires can do that as long as they have something to grasp onto. There I was, buck-naked, making my way down like a jungle monkey when the helicopter spotted me, and its speakers hollered at me to surrender. I had no choice but to jump from the seventh floor, and luckily I didn't land in a palm tree. That darn helicopter kept after me as I ran for cover, looking for somewhere to hide. And then the dogs came after me. Not a problem, as I can outrun them, but my fear was that I'd be cornered somewhere that I wouldn't be able to escape from. I ran like mad, scaring the hell out of the early-morning joggers.

"By then, at least two helicopters were keeping me in sight, and no matter where I ran or under what tree I hid, they found me. There was only one place that I couldn't be trapped in, and that was underwater. I ran as fast as I could, with the frickin' helicopters above me, until I reached Guanabara Bay, where I dove in and swam to the bottom. Lucky for us vampires, we can hold our breath for up to an hour or more. I swam underwater to the mouth of the bay, but the frickin' Brazilian Coast Guard had blocked it, and they were using sonar to detect me.

"Police speedboats soon arrived on the bay, and they threw hand grenades into the water to flush me out. Let me tell you, a hand grenade exploding underwater can kill even a vampire. I was lucky that they began near the spot where I had jumped in, and by then I was far enough away not to be harmed, but it would be just a matter of time before one was detonated near me. I didn't have to come up for air at that point, but eventually I would have to breathe, and the helicopters would have spotted me. With a long day's worth of light ahead of me, I had to find shelter fast.

"I found refuge in the Marina de Gloria, where I climbed aboard an unoccupied yacht and spent the day there. Luckily, it had plenty of rum onboard—I needed the energy. I found some clothes, too." She pointed with her thumb back at the bedroom, referring to the blue jumpsuit on the floor. "All day long, they searched for me in the bay. Even their Navy joined in. By nighttime, they gave up. They figured I was either dead or had managed to escape. At midnight, I looked out and spotted a cargo ship heading out to sea. Hoping that they'd let the ship sail through, I took my chances and swam underwater to that ship. I climbed into it and hid deep down in its bowels. They let it pass through the blockade and, as luck would have it, the ship was headed for New York City. A week later, here I am."

"That's horrible." I embraced her, glad to see her safe with me. "How do they know you are a vampire?"

"I was on the ship when I heard the captain telling the crew to watch out for hickeys on their necks and to report them immediately. He had been informed on how to spot the telltale signs of vampire bites. Dumb shits—as if vampires only bite on the neck! I sucked blood from everyone, including the captain, and they never knew where I bled them from."

The situation was serious. "What are you going to do?"

Angelique ran her hand through her fiery red hair. "Well, I need your help. I need to stay here until I can get myself back on my feet."

"Of course. That goes without saying," I reassured her. "But they know who you are. What will you do?"

"Yes, they do, and I need to figure out a new life and appearance for me. The sad truth is that I spent money faster than I was making it."

I didn't pry to find out how she made her money.

"The little I had put aside, I'm sure, was confiscated by the SNI. I'm penniless."

"No, you're not. You have me. You are my vampire sister." I hugged her again, and I felt her tension lessening. "How much do you need?"

"As I said, I need to get my life back on track and figure out what I'll be doing in the future. I just need money to buy some clothes for right now."

I knew there was a stash in this room in one of the drawers behind the bar. I checked in that drawer and, under the false bottom, I found bundles of cash. "Here is ten grand—help yourself to more if you need it." I tossed the stack to her. I pulled a debit card from my pocket and gave it to her as well. And from another drawer I pulled out a cellphone for her. "By the way, here is your old untraced cellphone."

Angelique had tears in her eyes. "I'm so glad you're my adopted sister."

"Me, too." We hugged again.

"I must get a new ID and see if I can change my appearance. I'll need to call François," she said.

"Good point. Ask him for his source of fake documents. We both may need them."

"OK." She looked at the phone. "I'll need to charge it first. Tell me, are Homeland Security and the NSA still spying on you?"

"They may monitor my cellphone and Internet communications, but I haven't seen anyone tailing me, and the apartment is free of bugs. Except for these Goths outside watching me."

Chapter 14. Offer of Help

"What Goths?"

"Remember Veronica Seyler?"

Angelique nodded.

"She joined a Goth cult that worships Dracula. They even have an Order of Dracula Society and a royal court. She's convinced them that Vlad is a vampire, perhaps Dracula himself. And she has an audio recording of the conversation Vlad had with Brenner the night of his capture. Even your name and Mundibuto's are mentioned on that recording. She and the Goth cult are trying to intimidate me by keeping watch on the front entrance of the Fifth Avenue apartment, and, of course, by trying to blackmail me."

I told Angelique the whole story.

"They don't have anything on you. They're just a bunch of losers."

"That's my conclusion, except for the cabbie. The biker woman killed him. They don't shy away from killing if needed."

"Are you even sure that the biker killed him?"

"You see, after I managed to evade her at Grand Central and get back into the same cab, she followed the cab again. I hid on the floor, and the biker gave up the pursuit. I asked the cabbie to take me to another subway station, and I came home."

"Did the biker see you getting back into the cab?"

"No, I don't think so. I think they placed a radio transmitter on me. Wait a second—" Something had just occurred to me. "The bug was in one of my boots."

Angelique furrowed her brows, puzzled.

"I took my boots off when I ran into Grand Central, and after I returned to the same cab I put my boots back on. The bug must have fallen out from one of the boots when I took them off. That's why the biker followed me again, but she gave up when she didn't see me in the cab."

"A radio transmitter? That's sophisticated."

"Uh-huh. The cabbie was shot while driving. Probably, the biker returned to following the cab, and when the poor man refused to stop to search for me, she shot him and he crashed. She didn't find me in the cab, but she found the transmitter on the floor and removed it."

"You've got guts to go in there to check them out." Angelique looked impressed. "And Veronica wonders who Angelique is after she hears my name on the recording."

"Yes. After the discussion with Veronica, I dismissed the PI. That's all he could have done, unless I went to the police."

"Are you going to the police?"

"No need. Not having any evidence to compromise me, they will give up their extortion plot. And I want to get Veronica without the police knowing about her whereabouts."

"Not to mention that if Veronica rats you out, it could put you back on their list of suspects for the East River limo murders."

"Could be," I agreed, but I was not worried about that.

"Would you like my help in nabbing Veronica?"

"I would, just to make sure that's all she knows and to take the recording and other evidence from her. But I need to go to Transylvania, and I don't have time for her."

"Nabbing people and destroying the evidence is my specialty, hon. Besides, we know where she is now. It won't take long. I think Goth will look good on me."

We burst out laughing. Angelique, as white as she was and with tinted black hair, would make an authentic Goth woman.

"Don't harm her," I told Angelique.

"You're going soft on the bitch who would have had you killed?"

"She's not worth killing."

"Very well," Angelique accepted. "By the way, when do you need to go to Transylvania?"

"Vlad gave me the dates of July 21st or August 22nd. It will be a full moon then, and I need to spread his ashes from the Sighisoara Clock Tower at midnight on either date. I'd like to do it as soon as possible."

"Full moon. Very dramatic."

"Do you have any idea why I need to spread his ashes at midnight on those particular dates?"

"No, but I think Mundibuto would know."

"But he's in Africa."

"François knows how to get in touch with him."

"I'll ask him next time I talk to him."

Angelique finished her drink. She needed sleep so I left her alone. Back in my Fifth Avenue apartment,

I checked on the watchers. They were at their stations. I expected them to have given up after my conversation with Veronica. Hadn't they read the memo?

Evening came, and two new Goth figures stood sentinel outside. Angelique would get to the bottom of this. Just as I thought about her, she came in.

"Hey, hon," she greeted me.

"Did you have a good sleep?"

"Yes, I'm back to normal. Are those the ones you were telling me about?" She pointed to the dark figures across the avenue.

"Yeah."

"I'll check them out. But first I might pay a visit to Pratt."

"The federal agent who kept watch on Vlad and me when Homeland Security was investigating?"

"The cute one, with the good-tasting blood." Angelique winked at me.

"Do you think it's safe?"

Chapter 15. Agent Pratt

Angelique dressed in black for the night and exited on the adjacent street. She checked out the two watchers in the park but decided to let them be for now. Pratt was on her mind and she missed him. She wondered why. Was it his blood or the sex? Maybe both. He might no longer be in New York if he was reassigned, but it was worth visiting his hotel just in case.

As she passed by the doors of a pub near the hotel, she heard Pratt's voice. She looked inside, but Pratt was with a blonde, having a drink. That was quick, courting another skirt, she thought. She didn't feel jealous. She left for Rio without saying goodbye. Everyone was entitled to his or her own life.

She debated whether to hang around and wait for Pratt, who might decide to take the blonde up to his room, or to just show herself briefly to see if Pratt would dump the blonde and see her. As it happened, Pratt was facing the windows of the pub and she made eye contact with him through a window before disappearing from his view.

He stood up as if he saw a ghost and then stormed out in the street. Outside, he looked in all directions, but Angelique was well hidden. He passed his hands through his hair several times, as if confused about what he'd seen or about what he'd do. The blonde came to the doorway, worried by his behavior. Dismissing any concern, he motioned with his hand and together they returned to their table. The chatting and drinking resumed, but Angelique detected uneasiness in Pratt's voice. He went to the men's room, while the blonde, after inspecting the small crowd in the pub, pulled her smartphone out and checked her messages, after which she began texting.

Angelique rolled her eyes in frustration. Everyone was instant messaging nowadays. What was wrong with a phone call, even a letter? Hell, people didn't even know how to write anymore, the way they used to when she was a human in France two centuries ago.

Pratt returned to the table and they continued chatting, but soon the conversation stalled and he wished the blonde goodnight. He stepped out into the street and looked up and down it, seemingly searching for Angelique, but she stayed hidden.

Shoving his hands into his pockets, he walked slowly down the street. She followed him from a distance. He must have had a lot on his mind as he walked the streets without a destination in sight. Occasionally he stopped and checked his messages on his phone and responded to some. After circling many blocks, he returned to his Midtown hotel. That was where Angelique wanted him to be, and she gave him five minutes to settle in.

The polite thing to do was to give him a call, which she did from the lobby. Pratt answered after the first ring. "Hello."

"Hi, Pratt. Guess who?"

"Is that you, Angelique? I thought I recognized you through the pub's window."

"That was me, honey. Care for a visit?"

"Sure. I'm in the same room. Come on up."

"I'll see you in two."

Two minutes later, Angelique was at his door. She detected the faint smell of perfume coming from his room. Maybe he put his hands on some woman or the blonde earlier, but she didn't care. She rapped on his door, surprised at how excited she was to see him. Pratt opened the door wide and invited her in. Only his mouth smiled, not his eyes. Angelique didn't waste a moment; she entered and embraced him.

The door behind her slammed shut. A gun cocked behind her head and she felt its cold barrel pressing at the base of her skull. "Freeze, or I'll shoot you," a woman's voice said from behind. The perfume scent was stronger now.

Chapter 16. Freeze or I'll Shoot You

Angelique had her arms around Pratt's neck. She gave him a quick bite and kiss on his lips, and looked him in the eyes. He stared coldly back at her, while jabbing his gun into her solar plexus. She didn't say anything and stared back at him. Trapped between two guns was inconvenient, even for a vampire.

"Pratt, what's the meaning of this?"

"You're under arrest, Angelique Brazeau."

She had never told him her last name, and she had suspected that he knew something about her real uniqueness. He knew she was a vampire. "Why are you arresting me, honey?"

"You've been identified for who you are."

"And who am I?"

"A possible suspect and a vampire."

"Shut up, Pratt," said the woman holding the gun behind Angelique's head. "Let's cuff this bitch."

"Were you the one who identified me, Pratt?"

He stared frostily into her eyes. "Special Agent Kelly took pictures of a whole bunch of you at Rockefeller Plaza. You were in them, too, and I identified you. With the help of an artist's rendering, our computers put your face together with your full identity. I finally learned why I was getting those hickeys on my neck. What kind of a freak was I sleeping with?" Pratt looked disgusted.

"I'm disappointed, Pratt. I liked you. But after this reception, there will be no future for us." She kiss-bit him again, while looking hypnotically into his eyes. He was in her possession.

"What the fuck? Pratt, what are you doing?" asked the woman from behind.

"I'm sorry, but I'll have to kill you," Angelique whispered in his ear. Pratt blinked dumbly. "Tell me everything, Pratt. Who are all the suspects your people identified?"

"You, Cat Sanders, François Le Beau, Veronica Seyler, Tiffani Arlin, and Miller, or Brenner."

"Tell me about François Le Beau."

"He's a suspect and a vampire like you. We believe he impersonated Dr. Le Bec and issued a fake death certificate for Vlad Draculesti."

"Why?"

"We don't know."

"Do you believe Vlad Draculesti is dead?"

"No."

"How about Veronica Seyler?"

"We, the FBI, and the NYPD are looking for her. She may shed some light on Miller's whereabouts."

"Why?"

"We believe Miller may have tried to blackmail Vlad."

"How about Tiffani Arlin?"

"We don't know about her, either."

"Do you know what happened to Miller?"

"No. We're still looking for him. Although he might be dead."

"Shut up," hissed the woman. "Raise your hands slowly and place them behind your head, lady."

"Is there an active investigation into Vlad and Cat Sanders?" Angelique asked.

"No. But they are persons of interest and are being monitored by the NSA."

"Goodbye, Pratt." She gave him one last kiss.

In less than the blink of an eye, Angelique slithered from in between them. The woman's gun ended up in Pratt's mouth, while his gun pointed to the woman's chest. Angelique shoved them together, and the impact caused both of them to pull the triggers. Simultaneous shots were fired.

Chapter 17. Death Is Not Pretty

The gunshot blasts from Pratt and the blonde were somewhat muffled by their close proximity, but they still made a big bang. The room was engulfed in blue smoke and a pungent smell. Pratt, his head blown off, dropped to the floor. The woman staggered backward and leaned against the door. Her white blouse was blackened by the gunfire, and a red circle was growing on her chest. She slowly slid to the floor, leaving a smear of blood on the door. Urine was pooling underneath her, and soon her blood mixed with it.

"Fuck," Angelique whispered.

The woman was the blonde from the pub. The bullet went through her and through the door. She was in a sitting position, propped up against the door, with her eyes wide open and blood trickling from the corners of her mouth. Pratt lay flat on his back, his mouth and cheeks torn by the gun blast. A pool of blood grew under his head. Brain pieces and blood splattered the walls.

Footsteps sounded outside the door. She couldn't waste any more time lingering there. She grabbed the blonde's purse and found her badge. She was a federal agent with Homeland Security, just like Pratt.

Angelique pulled the agent's phone out of the purse and placed it in her pocket. She retrieved Pratt's phone as well. Carefully, she moved away from the crime scene, trying not to step on any evidence of the crime.

Someone knocked on the door. The hole made by the bullet was large enough for an outsider to peer through and see inside the room. Angelique looked around for an escape route to get away without being seen. The door connecting to the next room was ajar. She walked quickly through it and entered into the other room, closing the door behind her. The air in this room smelled even more of the blonde's perfume. Pratt and the blonde must have had an affair. Angelique remembered a wedding band on the blonde's finger, but here they were, occupying two adjacent rooms with a connecting door between them—two cheating agents, screwing on assignment in the field. Not any better than the Secret Service boys.

Angelique cracked the door open and looked outside. There were several hotel guests clustered around, and a hotel employee was making her way to the door. The employee knocked and called out for someone inside to open the door, but the dead didn't respond. Using her master keycard, she unlocked the door and tried to open it, straining against the weight of the dead woman's body against it. She leaned her shoulder into it and slowly opened the door. The others crowded around for a better look.

Angelique didn't waste a moment and got out into the hallway, while the curious gaped at what they saw in the room. On her way to the elevator she pulled the fire alarm. The elevator doors opened just as she arrived there, and two more hotel employees burst out, as the fire alarm blared.

Swiftly she entered the elevator and descended to the lobby. Looking down so as not to make eye contact with anyone, she walked to the door marked "Employees Only" behind the check-in counter, which was now deserted, and went in. Quickly she scanned the room and found the "Security" door. It was locked. She knocked and heard someone rushing to the door. She took cover and waited to see who would come out. A fuzzy-haired geek opened the door and peeked outside. Not satisfied with what he saw, he walked to the exit door to observe the lobby. Angelique sneaked into the Security room without him seeing her.

The computers and security screens were in there. She went to the recorder and pulled out the DVD. On a nearby desk there was a container with blank DVDs. She took one and inserted it into the recorder's tray. On her way out, she spotted an electrical panel behind the door. Each switch was marked with a floor number. This was the electrical master-control panel for the entire hotel. Without hesitation she pulled the master switch down, and the entire hotel plunged into darkness.

More alarms began to sound as she walked into the lobby, now lit only by the emergency exit signs. People were running out of the dark lobby, while firemen and the police charged in. Angelique left the hotel and disappeared into the night.

Chapter 18. Something in the Blood

Angelique came over the next morning while I was having breakfast. I was surprised to see her up so early. Her eyes were red, not from blood lust but from crying. "Cat," she lamented.

"Angelique, what's the matter? Were you crying?"

She sighed heavily. "I really liked Pratt. But the sonofabitch was the one who ratted me out."

"What? How did he know all there is to know about you?"

"Agent Kelly took pictures of you and François when you were in Rockefeller Plaza with Miller, Veronica, and Tiffani."

I gasped. "I saw those pictures. Agent Kelly with Homeland Security showed them to me, but she didn't show me your picture."

"By coincidence, I was in some of those pictures, in the background. Probably at that time they hadn't identified me yet. Pratt recognized me and had an artist draw my picture, and from that drawing their computers identified me. That's how SNI knew about me, from the US intelligence agencies. François and I could be on all the 'dangerous person of interest' bulletins of intelligence agencies throughout the world. They suspect me of being a vampire—François as well—but I don't think they have any proof."

"That's terrible. They know about you worldwide?"

"Yes, because of Pratt. He and another woman agent tried to arrest me last night, and I caused them to shoot each other."

"Oh, my God! Federal agents?"

"Sorry. I liked the sonofabitch, but he wanted to be a hero, him and the blonde agent with whom he was having an affair—not that it mattered much. They were waiting for me in his room, and I found myself sandwiched between their guns."

"The FBI is going to be all over us."

"I don't think so, Cat. The FBI is going to be befuddled at what it discovers. The two of them shot each other at close range. Only they saw me, and I erased the messages and destroyed their phones, along with the security surveillance DVD from the hotel. Chances are good that no one saw me or can put me at the crime scene."

It was like déjà vu, killing people and misleading the authorities. I was hoping to avoid more killing, but maybe that was not possible anymore. Angelique liked the guy. She probably felt sorry for killing him, but she had no choice. Homeland Security and the FBI would have turned Manhattan upside down to find Angelique after Pratt reported seeing her. It was a terrible but unavoidable outcome.

"Are you OK?" I asked.

"Yeah. I'll be fine, in spite of my mishap."

I gave her a hug, and I felt that she appreciated having me near.

"Now, back to your stalkers," said Angelique, recovering. "I'll go out after them tonight."

"Please don't kill any of them," I pleaded.

"Of course not," she assured me. "I'll tint my hair black and dress up in black leather, studs, and chains. After I taste their blood, I'll pay a visit to the Silver Coffin after midnight."

"Be careful. They have surveillance cameras inside the club. It may be dark, but they're able to see."

"So am I. And I move very quickly."

Angelique left around eleven o'clock and crossed the avenue to the park. I watched her with my night-vision goggles, compliments of Vlad's arsenal. Mohawk on the left and Goose on the right were watching me tonight. Angelique approached Mohawk from his right, keeping behind a tree and staying out of Goose's view. Mohawk was leaning against the tree with his arms crossed. Striking as quickly as a venomous snake, Angelique reached from behind the tree and sank her fangs into the right side of the man's neck. His only reaction was to partly open his arms, but he remained frozen in place.

Her bite was quick, but she remained next to the man. She was probably asking him questions, and he told her everything she wanted to know. Vampire venom was good at making a man or a woman confess secrets. Satisfied with what she heard, she departed speedily, and, a few minutes later, she approached Goose from the opposite side, staying hidden from Mohawk's view.

I expected Angelique to bite her in the same manner, but something unexpected happened. Goose turned her head as if she heard someone from behind, and, instead of going for her neck, Angelique made full mouth contact with her. I knew that bite; I had seen Angelique administering that same bloody kiss to Agent Pratt many weeks ago, here in the park. Or maybe Angelique liked Goose? They remained briefly with their mouths interlocked, after which Angelique questioned Goose just as she did Mohawk. She then abandoned Goose and disappeared in the dark. The watchers remained at their posts, unaware of Angelique and of their chats with her.

To my surprise, Angelique returned.

"I thought you were going to the nightclub."

"Not tonight, Cat," she replied, making a sour face.

"What happened?"

"Those two have something in their blood that I don't like."

I looked at her, puzzled.

"I can taste whatever is in the victim's blood. If they smoke tobacco or pot, if they take legal or illegal drugs as well. Both of those two have something in their blood that I've never encountered before."

"Like what?"

"Some sort of chemical, which is affecting me as well."

"You mean you are immune to other drugs but not to what you found in these people's blood?"

"Yes. I'm immune to everything, drugs or diseases. But whatever is in their bloodstreams is making me groggy."

I remembered how Goose wasn't caught by surprise when Angelique went to bite her. "That's why . . ." I pointed to my mouth.

"Yes. I intended to bite her on the neck, but she heard me and turned her head. I wasn't quick enough, so instead I bit her on her lip."

"Do you feel alright?"

"Just a bit groggy and slow. I'm sure I'll purge the chemical out of my body with a drink." She went to the bar and filled a tall glass with gin.

"That will cure you?" I asked.

"The alcohol is my fuel, and I hope I'll burn off the chemicals faster this way." She took a drink. "That's why I abandoned my plans and decided to return. What in the hell are those people taking? I've never felt this way before." She shook her head as if to release a headache.

"I hope you'll feel better."

She nodded. "Interesting what they told me about their assignment."

"What did they tell you?"

"They are part of a following, the Order of Dracula, as you said. If Vlad only knew." She chuckled and took another drink. "They are just foot soldiers, carrying out whatever orders they get. In this case, they were told to shadow you at all times."

"Why?"

"They have not been told why. They're only soldiers. Most of the time, they deliver illegal drugs to pushers."

"Hmm. That place is involved with drugs. I kind of suspected it."

"These are synthetic drugs, made in labs around New York. I asked them about who the prince is.

They don't know, but the princesses are Melantha and Philomena."

"Why wouldn't they know who the prince is?"

"Apparently he stays in the dark or has a mask on when he addresses his followers, and the princesses carry out his orders and day-to-day duties."

"Bizarre. But then, what do you expect from a cult? False prophecies and mind-altering drugs. Did they say where they live?"

"Above the nightclub, as your PI suspected."

"Do they know Veronica?"

"Goose knew about her."

"How did Veronica get involved with these people?"

"She came seeking shelter."

I'm worried. "She said she was in possession of her father's files. God knows what else she's inherited from her father—how to contact Dr. Hellinherr, perhaps?"

"I wouldn't be surprised. The cult is perfect for the job of extortion." Angelique took another drink. "I'm feeling better. Tomorrow night, I'll pay the club a visit."

Chapter 19. At the Nightclub

It's midnight, and Angelique had waited patiently for the right opportunity to sneak inside the Silver Coffin Nightclub. The line to get in the nightclub was long. There were many people who were searching for the dark side of reality, where Angelique felt at home. The secretive prince and how he operated this business sparked the idea in Angelique's mind of opening a nightclub like this one and operating it from the shadows. She abandoned the thought as a limo stopped to unload a half-dozen VIPs. She needed to find a distraction to get in. A cat walked by, going to or coming from its feline business. Angelique grabbed the cat and petted it while approaching the entrance.

The group from the limo didn't seem to be hard-core Goth. They resembled tourists wanting to visit Gotham City's darkest nightclub. There were four women and two men, all Chinese. Angelique approached casually and, when the tourists were gathered around the bouncers, she hurled the cat into their midst. Momentary pandemonium erupted. No cat or humans were hurt, and it gave Angelique just the distraction she needed to sneak into the nightclub.

As a vampire, Angelique didn't need time to adjust her eyes to the darkness inside, and she walked unseen past the ticket booth and through the black curtains inside the club. The place reminded her of some of the better nightclubs in Berlin. She spotted bouncers with night-vision goggles standing in two opposite corners—smart, because the place was too dark for the average person to see much. She mingled with the crowd, while keeping her eyes on the bouncers. In no time she found her way to the staircase that led down to the Vampire's Lair.

The gatekeeper stood in front of the entrance with his arms crossed. It was dark enough and noisy enough that he didn't notice Angelique sneaking behind him and descending into the torch-lit chamber of the Vampire's Lair. As Cat had described it, the room did resemble a medieval chamber or a catacomb. There were several Goths in there, sitting and chatting quietly. The music was heavy metal and electronic Gregorian chants, not loud enough to raise the dead.

She passed by the silver coffin and sensed a smell of decay coming from it. The casket might contain an actual corpse, although embalmed with some mummifying chemicals. The place was getting more and more surprising and interesting. It occurred to her that she was by herself, without a date. Just about everyone was with a partner, either of the same or different sex. Most of the women were dressed in black evening gowns, with plenty of sparkling jewelry, some real, some faux.

"How are you tonight, Mistress? What would you like from the bar? A glass of blood, perhaps?"

Angelique eyed the waiter, a boyish, frail-looking young man with pimples on his face. "What kind of blood do you offer?"

"Goat for twenty dollars or human for one hundred dollars."

Angelique produced three fifty-dollar bills. "Human sounds interesting, and keep the change."

"It will be my pleasure to serve you, Mistress." He bowed.

They have high standards here, Angelique mused. She scanned the room and saw the wooden plank doors with heavy wrought-iron hinges at the other end of the chamber. Beyond those doors lay what she was interested in exploring.

The waiter returned with a crystal glass of blood on a silver tray. "Here you are, Mistress. Enjoy, and thank you." He bowed again, offering her the drink.

Angelique took the glass, smiled, and had a small sip. Crap. The blood was human, but it had the same drug in it that she tasted in the watchers' blood the previous night. This must be blood from one of those people. One sip was enough, but she smiled again at the waiter as if appreciating a fine vintage and walked away toward the other side of the chamber. As she passed by some of the tables, she noticed that most people were talking about money, sex, investments, sex, market opportunities, and sex, but nothing about death. Maybe these people were Wall Street brokers. She would need to get better acquainted with some of these freewheelers later on.

As she passed casually by the wood doors, she tried the handles. They were all locked. Maybe someone would go out or come in through them, so she sat down on a nearby chair, waiting patiently and pretending to sip her blood. The pimple-faced waiter walked by with a tray of drinks, pulled a key from his belt, and unlocked the door on the left. As he went in, Angelique saw a private party inside having a séance. Perhaps those other doors led to similar parlors, in which case there was nothing interesting inside them.

Just as she was assessing the situation, two ladies in black flowing gowns passed by her table toward the center door. One of them produced a key, unlocked it, and opened it to enter. There was a corridor behind that door. Bingo! That's where Angelique needed to explore. She moved quickly, pulled the debit card out of her purse, and placed it on the strike plate. The door was pulled close by one of the women, but the latch was blocked from engaging by the plastic card.

After listening for, but not hearing any more footsteps behind the door, Angelique opened it and entered. Inside she found herself in a semi-darkened corridor with a hefty and ornate wooden door at the end of it. Along the walls there were several other doors. She tried the first one but it was locked, and so was the second one, but the third door was unlocked. She cracked it open and peeked in, but it was empty and dark. It smelled like blood and urine in there. The blood smell was human and animal, mostly from cats. It could be where they extracted the blood they offered at the bar, but she couldn't identify any traces of goat blood.

The room was worth investigating. She stepped inside. Not much in there, except for a torture rack in the middle of the floor and a beheading block with an executioner's axe wedged into it. Streaks of dried blood ran down the stump, and more caked blood surrounded the base. Most of the urine smell came from under the rack, which was not for display but was an actual, functioning torture rack. She even spotted a human molar underneath it. The door was heavily padded to suppress any sounds, or screams, coming from the tortures carried out in there. There were no other doors or even a window out of that room. Angelique walked around the torture rack and sat in a high chair, admiring the décor and trying to make sense of this unusual place, right here in Manhattan.

Footsteps approached from the outside. For temporary cover, she moved quickly and stood flat against the wall behind the door. Someone opened the door halfway, and dim light came in from the corridor.

A woman said, "You left the door to the torture chamber unlocked, you turd."

"Very sorry, Princess Melantha. It wasn't me," a wimpy voice answered, which Angelique recognized as the waiter's. "Princess Philomena, I was with you all night in the Vampire's Lair."

"Yeah, Pink-Ass was with me all night, Melantha," said Philomena.

Ahh, so that was Pink-Ass! Angelique smiled.

Through the crack of the door she saw Philomena and Melantha. They were the two women she saw earlier coming through the door and the same ones Cat described. Without another word, they closed the door and locked her in.

Angelique was in no hurry to get out. Sure, the walls were made of concrete, but the door wasn't and she could break out. Or eventually someone would come in to let her out, unknowingly. She took her time to inspect the room in more detail, especially what was behind the sliding panels on the far wall. Behind them she found an excellent collection of medieval weapons: swords, crossbows, maces, axes, lances, and lots of knives. Most of the blades on these weapons were made of silver. Not silver-plated but pure silver, and she verified that by bending one of the knives.

Angelique smirked. Amateurs. Silver knives were too soft and would not penetrate the skin of any vampire. Whoever owned that arsenal had never met a real vampire, although they seemed to aspire to be vampire slayers. Everyone to his or her own illusion, she thought. However, she had no doubt that occasionally they tortured or even killed people in that room, or carried out occult rituals with animals. Many small ledges protruding from the walls held melted wax on them from candles lit in past rituals.

After checking the room thoroughly and finding lots of heavy chains and shackles, Angelique decided it was time to get out. The lock and the door were sturdy, and knocking it down would cause too much noise. Instead she picked up one of the hooks lying around and a mace and she removed the door hinge pins as quietly as possible. She pried the door open from the hinge side, squeezed out, and pulled the door back into its frame. Nobody would ever suspect that someone had entered that locked torture room, until they opened the door wide and it would come unhinged.

That Pink-Ass fellow would sure get a spanking after that.

As before, she was alone in the corridor, and she tried to open the other doors. They were all locked, including the ornate door at the end of the corridor. Just as she was about to give up and get out, she saw a white door opening. Someone was coming out.

Chapter 20. The Dispensary

A Goth man in a white lab coat came out through the white door and walked to another nearby door, unlocked it, and disappeared inside. Angelique was nowhere to be seen in the corridor, except up on the ceiling. She was with her back flat against the ceiling, propping herself up with her arms and legs between the walls of the narrow corridor. Just before the white door closed, she reached down with one foot and stopped it. After the man was gone, she kicked the door wide open, dropped down onto the floor, and went in.

Inside she found an all-white room, well lit by fluorescent light panels. It looked and smelled like a clinic or a laboratory. White tiles covered the floor and halfway up the walls. Glass-door cabinets loaded with hospital paraphernalia lined the walls. In the middle of the room there were two dentist-type chairs with overhead lights. Chains and hooks hung from pulleys on the ceiling. Their purpose escaped Angelique's understanding. She has seen such chains and hooks in abattoirs, but that wasn't a slaughterhouse. The dentist chairs had IV-bag holders and many sharp, pain-inflicting tools arranged on trays on side tables.

On the opposite wall there was a frosted-glass door, and Angelique tried to open it, but it was locked. There were too many locked doors around that place, to keep many secrets hidden. A lock pick would have come handy. She turned off the lights and sat in one of the dentist chairs in total darkness, listening. But other than some hints of the music from the main hall of the nightclub coming from above, there were no other human-made noises.

So far, she had found some disturbing evidence, but she hadn't found what she was looking for: Veronica, and how they intended to extort money from Cat. She could break a few doors down, but she didn't know which was the right door to break down, and the commotion would cause too much noise, alerting the people there to her intrusion. It seemed that she had to come back another night, when she would be better equipped. She leaned back, resigned to her futile incursion, when she saw a thin, dim line of light on the ceiling. That could be a ceiling panel, but what was behind it?

One of the chains was close enough to that crack, and she climbed up on it. As she suspected, it was a type of panel, a white-painted flat metal hatch that was latched from the other side. Even this darn thing was locked. In frustration, she hit the flat hatch and it buckled, coming loose and falling open, held by its hinges. A square shaft led up. At the very top a small bulb illuminated the interior. She grabbed the hatch's frame and pulled herself inside. The shaft was large enough to accommodate her hips and she had no problems climbing up, propping herself against the walls with her legs and her back while scooting upward.

At the top she pushed up another hatch located on the floor of a new room, and peeked in. It was an office, judging by the desk and the leather chair nearby. She climbed up inside the room. Dim light came through a frosted-glass door. The walls were lined with shelves loaded with glass jars that were filled with a white substance. What was this room? Why have such a shaft between this room and the clinic below? The mystery was somewhat resolved when she noticed the pulley and chains on the ceiling of this room. It was a delivery chute. This was a storeroom of some kind. Angelique unscrewed the lid on one of the jars from the shelves and sniffed the thick white liquid. It contained the same substance that she tasted in the blood of the watchers and in the glass of blood from the bar. It also smelled of something flammable, probably the base of this substance.

The door of this room was not locked. She opened the door and looked into a hallway with many apartment doors. Round ceiling lamps lit this corridor. Through the window at the end of the hall, she saw the iron fire-escape stairs dimly lit by the streetlights. At least she found one escape route, if needed. The sign on the storeroom's glass door read "Dispensary." The white paste in the jars was probably what was dished out to the occupants of these apartments.

She returned to the dispensary and closed the door behind her. One mystery was unraveling. Whatever that white stuff was, the watchers took it, making them substance-dependent. No wonder they called themselves soldiers. This was a good way to have an army that does whatever you want them to do, including watching Cat's apartment entrance. Besides their ongoing venture, Cat was their main objective now.

"Is anyone in here?" came a voice from down below through the shaft. "Why are the lights shut off?"

That voice sounded familiar. It was Veronica.

Chapter 21. Finding Veronica

Without hesitation, Angelique grabbed the chain's hook above and lowered herself down the shaft, bursting through the clinic's ceiling and landing on the white tile floor. She let go of the chain and it retracted back into the ceiling, after which the ceiling panel banged shut. Standing between the two dentist chairs, she was alone in the fully lit room. Veronica wasn't there. Darn it! She missed her.

A faint metal sound came from the knob on the corridor door. Angelique regretted letting the chain retract. Quickly, she ran and flattened herself against the wall behind the door. It worked in the torture room and it should work again, except that the lights were on, and they were bright. Through the crack of the open door on the hinge side she saw Princesses Melantha and Philomena. They stood in the doorway, inspecting the clinic. Apparently satisfied with the condition of the room, they entered and shut the door behind them, without turning to look back. They walked to the opposite end of the room to the other door, where they stopped, and as they turned, each one pulled an Uzi from the folds of her evening gown and pointed it at Angelique.

Impressive! Considering the drawn weapons, they must have known about her intrusion. Melantha and Philomena exchanged cold glares with Angelique. The guns didn't intimidate Angelique, but she had to take the women down before they fired. She was quick, but not quicker than bullets coming at her. She tensed, about to strike.

"You must be the real Angelique," said either Philomena or Melantha. Angelique didn't know who was who. "Oh, pardon me. I don't mean to be impolite. I am Princess Philomena, and this is Princess Melantha." Philomena had a sickening, syrupy smile. Melantha glared, ready to kill.

"Aiming your guns at me is very impolite," Angelique said calmly.

"May I remind you that you are trespassing?" Philomena said.

"Did Cat send you here to find Veronica?" Melantha asked without any pleasantries. This one was more to Angelique's liking—straight to the point, rude, and delicious to kill.

"Maybe," said Angelique, trying to figure out their game plan.

"Would you like to see her, Angelique?" Philomena asked.

"Where are you hiding her?"

"Hiding? We're not hiding her," said Philomena. "Would you like to see her?"

Without waiting for a reply from Angelique, Melantha shouted over her shoulder, "Veronica, come in."

The door behind the two opened and Veronica came in. She was dressed in white pants and a green T-shirt, very Goth-inappropriate. Her blue eyes scrutinized Angelique.

"Who are you?" Angelique asked, playing ignorant, although she knew Veronica.

"I'm Veronica, formerly Cat's friend. So you are the Angelique who 'bagged' my father."

"What gives you that idea?"

"You are that Angelique." Veronica pointed an accusatory finger at her.

"Stop playing games," Melantha said.

"You are my father's killer," said Veronica, narrowing her eyes. "Cat will pay big to keep my mouth shut, and she'll have to pay double to get you back. Or maybe I should keep you and slay you slowly." She grinned.

"Have you ever slain anyone before, Veronica?" Angelique stepped closer to them, observing that Philomena and Melantha's arms had drooped, tiring from the effort of holding up the heavy Uzis.

"That's none of your business. But I know I'll enjoy killing you. Melantha, Philomena, put your guns down. I'm going to get this bitch by myself." She raised her hands as if ready to attack.

Angelique laughed. Her eyes became bloodshot, and blue veins pulsated on her forehead; she was halfway to showing her vampire face. Veronica screamed but stood her ground. Angelique wouldn't let her get away this time, and since the Uzis were pointing at the floor, she was ready to pounce.

Without warning, the floor collapsed underneath Angelique, and she found herself falling.

Chapter 22. Trapped

Falling was not a big concern for Angelique, other than what was waiting for her below. She splashed into a tub of thick muck, which softened her fall, and she sank slowly before touching bottom. With a solid base under her feet, she immediately tried to jump out, but that didn't work. She rose only up to her waist before sinking back down. She tried again, but it was more difficult the second time around. It was as if this gray goo was thickening. Up to her neck in the stuff, she tried to move to the edge to pull herself out, and she managed to get a grasp of the tub's rim with her right hand. But that's as far as she got. Her left arm was just below the surface, but she couldn't lift it out of the gray compound, which was hardening fast. With one last effort, she pulled with her right arm to free herself, but she only managed to break off part of the tub's rim.

She was trapped in an epoxy compound that was becoming hard cement faster than one could draw a breath, which reminded her to draw one big breath and hold it to make sure she would not be constricted by the hardening epoxy and eventually suffocate. Five minutes later, as the epoxy's temperature increased, it hardened completely.

Angelique examined her situation. She was encased in cement, with only her right hand free. Up to her neck in this stuff, she could only move her head. Her left arm and her body were completely inside the cement. After she exhaled, she had a larger cavity around her torso, and at least she was able to breathe without restriction.

The floor above closed and the room plunged into darkness. This was the first time she had ever been trapped and incapacitated in such a complete manner. How she wished she had both of her arms free! She felt like a pinned butterfly, immobilized and unable to do a thing about it. Breathing slowly to calm herself down, she scrutinized the room they had trapped her in. It was a large concrete-block room as big as the clinic above. Stainless steel mixers of a medium size cluttered some of the benches against one wall. Many other stainless steel and glass lab containers were arranged on a rack. A distiller, evaporators, and an oven stood on her left side. Several other fiberglass vats, smaller than the one she was in, were located randomly in the room. Bags and boxes of supplies and empty glass jars lined the shelves on another wall. It looked like a bakery, but it was a chemical lab. This was where the drugs were cooked.

Angelique debated with herself whether to scream and let her frustration blow, but it would be futile since there was nothing she could do at this time. Only Cat knew her whereabouts, but could she rescue her? Cat was not a vampire, and it was doubtful that she could come to her rescue, while she was encased in a frickin' epoxy block. Finally, she screamed from the top of her lungs. And then there was silence.

The neon tube lights flickered on; someone was about to pay her a visit. A ceiling door opened and collapsing stairs unfolded to the floor. A muscular Goth woman with spiky black hair descended first. She held a .38 revolver in her right hand and a short samurai sword in the other. Her mean eyes glowering, she approached Angelique cautiously, the gun pointing at her. She circled the tub, while Angelique rotated her head as far as she could to keep an eye on the new nemesis. Once behind Angelique, where she couldn't be seen, she tapped her sword on the surface of the hardened epoxy. It sounded the same as tapping on concrete.

She walked in front of Angelique and smirked. "Trapped, aren't you?"

"Who are you?" Angelique asked.

"I'm Nisha. I'm the executioner around here. And you are Angelique. Veronica says that you are a vampire. Is that true?"

"Nonsense. There are no such things as vampires. That's just a legend. Get me out of here!"

"We'll have to cut you out with a diamond blade. You're not a vampire?" Nisha looked disappointed.

"What's the meaning of this? Cut me out of here!" Angelique played indignant, as if she were any other society lady who happened to be trapped in epoxy.

"Not yet. First I want to see if you bleed." Swiftly, Nisha slashed at Angelique's hand, except that Angelique caught the blade. Nisha was taken aback. No one could touch a razor-sharp samurai blade and not be cut. Angelique held the blade in her hand but didn't bleed. Nisha pulled and twisted the sword, but couldn't get it out of her grip, and there was not a drop of blood to be seen. There they were, Nisha holding the sword by the hilt and Angelique holding it by the blade, and neither one was willing to let go.

Nisha pointed the gun at Angelique's head. "Let my blade go or I'll pop you."

Angelique looked down the barrel. This Nisha had the eyes of a killer. She was not the bluffing type. "If you don't try to cut me again, I'll let it go."

Nisha nodded and Angelique opened her hand, but the blade broke at the point where she held it. Angelique's palm had no cuts on it, just blue lines.

"What the hell are you?" Nisha whispered in shock to see her sword broken.

"A vampire," said Veronica as she descended into the room, followed by Melantha and Philomena. "A real vampire. My dad was right. Where is Vlad?"

"Who?"

"Vlad Draculesti. Dracula. The one who told you to bag my father."

"He's dead."

"That's what everyone says. But we've got you." Veronica smiled meanly.

A Goth man came down into the room as well and approached Angelique. "The question is, what do we do with a vampire?"

"And who are you?" Angelique asked.

"I'm the Prince."

"The Prince?" said Angelique. "Why weren't you the first one to come down and check on me?"

"Because I'm a prince and I have specialists who do that. Nisha here loves to torture and kill people. You will be the first vampire to scream at her hands."

Nisha caressed her chin with the barrel of her gun. Angelique sighed. Amateur, she thought.

"Therefore," said the Prince, walking around Angelique with his hands clasped behind his back. "What should we do with you? Only your head and one of your hands are above the epoxy cement. I suppose we could cut them off and see what's in your blood. Hmm?"

"She's tough. She broke my blade and did not get cut," said Nisha.

The Prince raised his eyebrows in delighted surprise. "In that case, I want you whole, and I'll make you my slave. My vampire slave."

Chapter 23. White Fog

"Your slave? My ass!" smirked Angelique.

"Bring the tools," the Prince told Nisha. While she busied herself looking for the tools, the Prince said, "You'll be surprised how soon you'll be my slave. I've concocted a drug so potent, so addictive, that whomever I give it to, they become my slaves and do whatever I tell them to do."

"How did you manage to make that?" Angelique asked.

"I'm a chemist, or rather, I used to be a chemist, working at a 40-hour-a-week job for a big chemical corporation, making peanuts like everyone else. One day it occurred to me that I could engineer some new drugs that could be as potent as meth, but without the difficulties and dangers novices encounter when they cook the drugs. I quit my day job, and soon I was a drug producer.

"I found out quickly the difficulties in distribution and sales that every new businessman faces. I approached gangs to sell my product to them, but they either thought I was the police, entrapping them, or they got greedy and wanted me to work for them. Imagine—exchanging one employer for another, and a less reputable one, at that. I wasn't about to have a shoot-out with all those losers, so I stayed low for a while, selling my new meth to established clients through this nightclub. The owner, Sabien Salem, took a cut, and the business was OK but not spectacular.

"I figured I needed my own soldiers—dedicated, loyal, and obedient. Soldiers who would kill for me, or be killed, if necessary, and not rat me out if they were caught by the police or rival gangs. I created a new drug that would make any man or woman my slave, servant, soldier. I call it White Fog. Whoever takes it forgets who they are, and I, the Prince, become their god. We make White Fog and all our synthetic drugs right in here." He motioned around the basement. "And you saw the Dispensary upstairs, where the finished products are stored. My own foot soldiers distribute my products, and occasionally I enslave other gangs to work for me."

"Who's the stiff in the silver coffin?"

"Sabien Salem, the former owner of the Silver Coffin. I made him my slave, and after he transferred ownership of the nightclub to me, I had no more use for him. I preserved him like a mummy and kept him as a trophy. White Fog has a huge potential. I used it on the little old lady who owns this building. I control her estate and I practically own this building. Before Veronica Seyler came around asking for shelter and proposing her plans of getting money from Cat Sanders, I was about to expand into Wall Street. Those brokers and bankers are easy prey for enslavement. I'm sure you saw some of them in the Vampire Lair's lounge."

"It seems you have plenty of money. Why go after Cat Sander's money?"

"Money is good, more money is better, and all the money is godly. I haven't initiated my Wall Street takeover yet. And I've just started in the wholesale drug business. I need capital to grow fast, before some drug cartel from Mexico destroys me. I'll

122

destroy them instead, and I'll become the drug king of the US and eventually the world. I concoct drugs a junkie could only dream of. And the drugs don't have to be transported or smuggled. A small lab like this can make them anywhere the market is located, with local ingredients. Like here in Manhattan. Maybe I'll start a franchise." He looked thoughtful, inspired by his brilliant new marketing idea.

"Veronica seems to have come along at a good time," said Angelique.

"Veronica? Oh, yes. She wants money. I want money. Win-win. However, I have to confess, it's the vampire potential that she brought to the table that sparked my imagination even more. If it is true—and it is true, judging by your presence here—vampire blood is the Holy Grail. Imagine being a vampire, living forever and being rich beyond belief." The Prince closed his eyes and inhaled deeply to savor his new future.

"Pink-Ass!" Nisha shouted toward the ceiling door. "Where is the insemination tool?"

Angelique raised her eyebrows.

The Prince observed her questioning look. "Insemination tool is a name Pink-Ass coined. That retarded serial killer has a sense of humor. For some reason, not everyone I want or need to be my slave will take the elixir. I devised a tool that will force it down anyone's throat, and yours, too." One corner of his mouth rose in a smirk.

Angelique looked at Veronica. "Did you take White Fog?"

She shook her head but said, "That's none of your business."

"You are an extortionist."

"You bet," Veronica conceded with a smile. "The Prince and I have a business arrangement. I get Cat Sanders entrapped and blackmail her. She pays through the nose, and we may let her live."

Pink-Ass came down with a case in his hand. "Prince, can I do it?" His voice trembled with excitement.

Angelique ignored Pink-Ass, and she asked Veronica, "What makes you think the Prince needs you anymore? He can get money from Cat without your help."

"Sure, Manhattan is full of billionaires, but getting money out of them is hard. And so it is with Cat Sanders. She can afford a lot of protection, and we won't be able to get near her. But I have the incriminating evidence that will make her give away all her money."

Pink-Ass placed the container next to Angelique's head and opened it. Meticulously, he removed a funnel, a face harness, an electric drill, and what looked like a small roto-rooter. He bent down close to Angelique's face, ready to place the harness on her head. He got too close and Angelique, with a hammering jerk, head-butted him. His nose flattened and blood squirted out of it as if a tomato had been squished. He leaned back, screaming in pain from the top of his lungs, while holding his hands over his demolished nose. Tears and blood poured over his shirt. Nisha laughed, pointing to

Pink-Ass. Melantha and Philomena placed their hands on their hips, not amused.

"Why did you have to head-butt him?" Philomena asked furiously.

"He's lucky he's alive." Just as Angelique said that, Pink-Ass collapsed.

"Enough of this bullshit," said Melantha. "If Cat Sanders does not listen to reason, now that we have you, how much will she pay us to free you?"

"She'll pay nothing."

"We'll find out, won't we?"

"Prince, get me out of this epoxy straightjacket immediately," demanded Angelique.

Everyone in the basement erupted in hysterical laughter, except for Pink-Ass, who was flat on the floor, and Angelique.

The Prince came over to Angelique's side and opened a jar of White Fog. He spooned the drug, which resembled sour cream, from the jar and held it in front of Angelique's mouth. "You don't have any say over what we do or don't do. But if you're a good girl and swallow this spoonful of White Fog, then and only then we'll cut you free. Open wide." He pushed the spoon forward. Angelique turned her head.

"Nisha, let's use the insemination tool." The Prince motioned toward Angelique. "And be careful—she's still capable of biting."

Nisha moved behind her. Angelique struggled but couldn't keep Nisha from putting the face harness on her head. Next, Nisha attached the funnel to the brackets in front of the mouth. The tip of the funnel was in front of Angelique's lips. Nisha attached the electric drill to the roto-rooter and sneered as she shoved the flexible snake wire down the funnel toward her mouth.

"Well, Angelique," said the Prince. "Want it or not, I'm going to bore down your throat and shove the White Fog into you."

Chapter 24. Liberated

The Prince dropped a spoonful of White Fog into the funnel and motioned with his head to Nisha to begin. She smiled, anticipating the torment Angelique would face. She pulled the trigger on the electric drill and fed in the snake. Melantha and Philomena got closer to watch, their eyes hungry to see pain and convulsing.

The snake advanced, but suddenly it began contorting and twisting into a bundle. The funnel twisted and ripped off the facial harness. Panicking, Nisha dropped the still rotating drill, which fell on the top of the epoxy cement and came slowly to a stop, tangled in the funnel and the snake wire.

"What the hell happened?" the Prince screamed at Nisha. "How did you screw this up?" He pointed indignantly to the mangled mess of his insemination tool.

"I did what I usually do. I don't know what happened!"

Melantha picked up the funnel and inspected it. "This bitch bit the tip of the funnel and constricted the snake so it wouldn't go through."

Angelique spat out a piece of metal.

"You know what, Angelique? You're too much trouble," said the Prince. "We'll let you stay encased in there. It's safer that way."

Philomena ran a hand over the Prince's shoulder and then leaned on her elbows in front of Angelique, at a safe distance. With a syrupy smile, she said, "Angelique. I don't know what freak of nature or laboratory you are, but you are locked inside a solid block. Other than your hand and your head, you cannot even twitch. Stay where you are until we get what we want, or drink the fucking elixir and we'll cut you out of this block. It is up to you." She straightened up and crossed her arms.

Angelique bit her lower lip and inhaled. She was trapped and they were in control. "OK, you win. I'll drink your drug if you cut me out of this. I cannot breathe. I'm going to die." Her face distorted in anguish and pain.

Philomena looked at the Prince, and he smiled, satisfied. He scooped up another spoonful of White Fog and shoved it toward Angelique. She opened her mouth, swallowed the white cream, and grimaced in disgust.

"Nisha, get the chains, the shackles, and the circular saw," said the Prince. "I want her intact."

Nisha walked by Pink-Ass and kicked him. "Get up, loser." Pink-Ass stirred, awakened, and sat up. He wailed, touching his nose tenderly. "Stop your crying. We have work to do," admonished Nisha, who grabbed him by the back of his neck and stood him up. Sheepishly, he followed her up the stairs.

A few minutes later, they returned, bringing the chains and shackles from the torture room along with a circular saw. The Prince, Veronica, and Philomena left the room, uninterested or unwilling to participate in the messy extraction. Only Melantha remained behind, filing her nails. Angelique seemed to be under the drug's influence, her eyelids halfway closed.

Melantha smirked and pointed to Angelique. "That shit works on everyone."

"Maybe," said Nisha, "but I'm not getting close to her without making sure she is chained and secure. Pink-Ass, hang this chain on that hook." She pointed to a hook on the ceiling.

They collared her first and hooked the chain attached to the steel collar to the ceiling hook. Next they shackled her right hand and connected the chain to the collar.

Melantha seemed satisfied with the progress and left the room, closing the ceiling door behind her.

Pink-Ass turned on the diamond-blade circular saw. "What if I cut your nose off?" He brought the spinning saw closer to Angelique's face.

"Give me that! Idiot." Nisha snapped the saw away from Pink-Ass. "Prince wants her intact. Got that?" She waved a finger in his face. "Get ready for dust," she said, as she turned on the exhaust fan.

Angelique closed her eyes and held her breath. Nisha began cutting. The saw made teeth-jarring noise, and the room filled with dust. They cut and liberated her left wrist first, which they placed in another shackle and attached the chain to the collar. They freed both her arms and tightened the chain, keeping Angelique's arms pulled up toward the ceiling.

"Water break," said Nisha after a while.

Pink-Ass and Nisha sat down on nearby plastic chairs and drank from water bottles.

"We should give her some water," said Pink-Ass. "Poor thing must be parched." Nisha shrugged. He walked to Angelique and poured his bottle of water over her head.

Angelique shook her head to get rid of the water and said, "No thanks, but I could use a stiff drink, though."

Pink-Ass looked wide-eyed at Nisha. "Alcohol will mellow her even more. Right?"

"You aren't as stupid as you look. There is some pure alcohol in that bottle." She pointed to a gallon glass bottle on one of the shelves.

Pink-Ass shuffled over to the shelf and returned with the bottle, uncapped it, and said, "Now, let's not have any funny business here. Open your mouth." Angelique opened her mouth obediently, and Pink-Ass poured the alcohol down her throat. She drank half the bottle, to the surprise of Nisha and Pink-Ass. As they expected, Angelique's head drooped. She was out. Or at least that's what they thought.

The Prince came in to check on the progress.

"She's asleep. We gave her some of that alcohol," said Pink-Ass.

He looked at Angelique and then at the bottle. "She drank that much? That would kill a man." The Prince lifted Angelique's eyelids. She was out but alive.

"I doubt it," said Nisha. "Do you think she's a real vampire?"

"Let's extract her from the block and we'll find out," he said.

"Her body will be difficult to pull out," said Nisha, rubbing the back of her neck.

"What if we cut grooves in the cement, pound wedges in them, and crack the block open?" Pink-Ass suggested.

The Prince and Nisha looked at each other, surprised.

"Who knew Pink-Ass was a logger?" wondered the Prince out loud.

"I was. I really was. I cut a few bitches in half with a chain saw after I raped them." Pink-Ass gave an idiotic smile.

"I didn't mean that kind of logger," said the Prince as he walked up the stairs to leave. "Get back to work."

Suddenly Pink-Ass gained status in Nisha's eyes. The stupid boy was a serial rapist and killer. For the moment, she was impressed.

They proceeded as Pink-Ass suggested, and, after cutting and pounding wedges for hours, they liberated her torso, and then one leg, which they shackled, and then the other leg after it was freed from the epoxy. Angelique hung from the chains above the floor, half-conscious.

"Go and get the Prince," Nisha told Pink-Ass.

The Prince returned with Melantha and admired Angelique hanging limply by the chains. "I don't feel safe with her restrained just by chains. What do you think, Melantha?"

"Yeah, she's dangerous. What if we strap her on the rack?"

"The torture rack? Why not? It will make for an ideal display." He motioned with his head to Nisha and Pink-Ass to bring the rack from the torture chamber.

Melantha checked the chains. They were sturdy enough to restrain a gorilla, but she looked unconvinced. "I don't think the chains will be enough to keep her down. We should kill her."

The Prince cocked his head and pointed to the chunks of epoxy cement with patterns left from Angelique's body. "That may have been the best restraint. You know, I have some acrylic sheets that soften when heated and harden when they cool. I can wrap her like a cocoon." He walked to one of racks, pulled out a plastic sheet, and showed it to Melantha. She approved.

Nisha and Pink-Ass brought the rack down and placed it on the floor, breathing heavily.

"We need to lower her onto the rack," said the Prince. "Pull her arms straight over her head and tie the chain at one end. Pull her legs straight and tie the chain at the other end. Then I'll place acrylic sheets on her and heat them to mold them to her body." He pulled several acrylic sheets out from the storage rack along with a plumbing gas torch, ready for the work at hand.

"Pink-Ass," said Nisha. "You grab the chains on her arms and I'll grab the chains on her feet. We'll take her down and place her on the rack, and then tie her. Ready?"

The two of them heaved her body and struggled to place her on the rack, when suddenly, Angelique came back to life. She wrapped the arm chains around Pink-Ass's neck, and he collapsed under her. She shook the chains tied to her legs and Nisha flew backward from the whipping chain.

Angelique kicked Pink-Ass out of the way and stood up. Her arms were chained at the wrists and connected to the neck collar, but she had plenty of slack to move her arms. Her ankles were shackled, but that wouldn't keep her from jumping. She looked pissed.

Melantha screamed.

"Shoot her, Nisha!" ordered the Prince.

Nisha pulled her gun out from the holster and shot Angelique twice in the stomach.

Chapter 25. Pay Up or Else

The phone woke me up. The caller ID displayed "unknown caller," but I answered anyway. "Hello?"

"Hello, Cat," Veronica replied.

I was confused. Veronica's calling me? I thought that Angelique had taken care of her. Or maybe she was on the run and wanted to keep in touch. "What do you want, Veronica?"

She giggled. "A shit load of money, Cat."

"Why would I do that?"

"You will if you want to see Angelique again."

"What? You're bluffing."

"I just sent you a photo of her. I'll call you back in five, after you recover from your shock."

I didn't wait for a call back. I called Angelique's phone while running to the Red Apartment. The phone rang several times until I made a connection. "Hello, Cat," Veronica answered instead. "Have you received the picture yet?"

"How did you get her phone?" I opened the secret door and ran to Angelique's bedroom. It was empty.

"Didn't I tell you that I have her?"

"You have her?" I put the call on hold and reviewed the messages. There was Angelique's picture. It was just a headshot, and she looked distraught. I connected back to Veronica. "Hello."

"Convinced we have her?"

"Let me talk to her."

"She's indisposed right now. But she'll be up to her usual self by ten tonight. That's when you'll visit us and pay up."

I could feel my blood pressure rising. They've got Angelique and somehow they have drugged her. I was in no position to negotiate, other than to pay whatever they asked. "Why at ten? Why not right now?"

"We'll tell you when and where to come. And bring all your bank accounts to make wire transfers."

"How much do you want?"

"Your whole fortune, of course."

"Don't be ridiculous. Not all that I have sits in cash at the bank."

"I know. Tonight, you'll make a goodwill deposit of fifty billion dollars, otherwise we'll kill Angelique."

"Don't you dare touch her!"

"Or maybe we will give her to a certain Dr. Hellinherr. I bet he'll pay good money for a real vampire."

I screamed in frustration. She knew about Dr. Hellinherr. That was bad, and I gave myself away through my emotions.

"Now, now. No need to be hysterical. You do what I tell you and you'll get your freak friend back."

"What did you do to her?"

"Nothing much. Anyhoo, I'll call you before ten and give you instructions on how to visit us. And don't forget those account numbers."

"If you touch her, you're dead."

"Heh, heh, heh. Goodbye."

She disconnected. I fell to my knees and started crying. What could I do? I could ask for help from my other two vampire friends, François and

Mundibuto, but I could reach only François by phone. I called him immediately and left a voice message to call me back urgently.

François called me a half-hour later. "*Cherie*, what is the problem?"

"Thank God, you got my message. Angelique has been taken hostage by Veronica and her gang."

"Where?"

"Here in New York."

"What is she doing in New York?"

"Didn't she call you and tell you what happened in Rio?"

"No."

"Where are you now?"

"I'm in Singapore."

"Oh, crap. You're too far away. And Mundibuto is in Africa." I sighed, feeling hopeless. "Angelique was taken captive, and they want a ransom for her by ten o'clock tonight. The money is no problem, but I doubt they'll let her go."

"I'll charter a plane, but it will take a day to get to New York. Mundibuto will take at least two days to get there."

"Hurry! I'll try to delay if I can. I don't want Angelique harmed. Veronica knows of Dr. Hellinherr, and I'm sure she'll contact him."

"*Merde*. I'm going to kill them all."

And that was a promise, knowing firsthand how François the vampire had dealt with my kidnappers the last time.

I was on my own until at least one, if not two, of the vampires arrived in New York. In the meanwhile, I would have to play along. Paying the money was not the issue, even if I had to give all my money away to save Angelique. I was afraid for Angelique, and most of all, I was afraid that Angelique would end up on Hellinherr's dissection table. That evil family would finally get vampire blood and continue their efforts to create a super race.

I paused and touched the bump under my right ear. That was where François implanted the ampule containing the drop of vampire blood Vlad gave me. Should I break it, let the vampire blood infect me, and become a vampire myself? I didn't think this situation would ever arise. But maybe this was that situation? I didn't have to rush things. Vlad had told me that, within a few seconds, the blue vampire blood would begin to work, and I would become stronger and faster. And then, within 24 hours, I would be transformed into a full vampire—fangs and all.

And then I had my Strigoi. But they were only going to protect me if someone tried to harm me. They wouldn't attack anyone unless I were in danger. I was not so sure about how effective they were going to be, anyway. I only experienced their presence once, when I accidentally hurt myself. Would they come to my aid if no one hurt me? And if they appeared, how would I ask them to kick ass?

I rubbed my face with my hands and inhaled deeply to shake my anxiety. They wanted my money. All of it. And if they would get all of it, would they let me go? Afterward, if I were poor, I wouldn't be a problem for them, other than being a witness. For sure, my chances would be slim of being left alive after they sucked all my money out of me. They were vampire bloodsuckers, as well as being vampire slayers.

Somehow, they'd managed to immobilize a vampire. That was not impossible, but it was very difficult to do. After the ransom was paid, letting Angelique walk away would be the same as letting go of the tiger's tail. She would return and kill them. They would either kill her or sell her to Dr. Hellinherr. Or keep her for their own needs, perhaps becoming vampires themselves.

Knowing the worst and most likely outcome simplified my decision. I'd go in, and I'd either die or come out alive with Angelique.

Chapter 26. Dr. Hellinherr

Veronica punched in the numbers for Dr. Hellinherr.

"Hello," a grumpy voice answered.

"Hello, Dr. Hellinherr. This is Veronica, Miller's daughter."

"Miller's daughter?"

"Yes, I'm his daughter, Veronica. According to his notes, he wanted to make a business deal with you."

"What business deal?"

"He proposed bringing you a vampire."

"A vampire!" The man laughed. "The stuff of legends."

"Well, I have such a creature in my possession. My dad told me that you were very much interested in the blue blood of vampires. Still interested?"

"Where's Miller? Why hasn't he called me back? It has been almost two months since he told me his cockamamie proposal. And then he goes silent."

"He was killed trying to capture the vampire Vlad Draculesti."

"What? Vlad Draculesti? But he died."

"Maybe. I am not sure if Vlad is really dead, but I have in my possession a female vampire."

Dr. Hellinherr paused for a moment. "What are you proposing?"

"The same thing my dad proposed last time. Except this time I have the goods, and you can come and inspect her yourself."

"Are you sure this is not a hoax?"

"I've got the real deal."

"Continue."

"My dad asked you for a 50-50 partnership for a vampire, subject to your verification."

"To verify that you have a real vampire captive, I'd need to extract her blood and analyze it in my lab."

"You can analyze her and her blood only at our location. The blood does not leave the premises until we have the necessary paperwork drawn."

"Hmm. Then I'll have to bring my equipment."

"We'll provide you with all the equipment you need. Of course, making her bleed is another story."

"What do you mean?"

"She has tough skin."

"When can we come and see her?"

"We?"

"Well, yes, I'll be accompanied by my associates."

Veronica took some time to respond. "You're allowed one associate. We'll call you tomorrow to schedule the visit. We're in Manhattan."

"New York? Tomorrow? Why the rush?"

"She's not getting any fresher."

"You didn't say she was dead."

"We're not sure."

"Very well then. I'll arrive in Manhattan tomorrow morning."

After Veronica disconnected, the Prince asked, "Tell me again—who is this Dr. Hellinherr?"

"According to my dad, Dr. Hellinherr Sr., an Austrian, was convinced that vampires exist. He wanted to capture a vampire and experiment with the blood to create an eternal youth serum. He worked with Hitler and Stalin, separately, to create a super race. The Hellinherrs came to America and continued research on the fountain of youth. Hellinherr Senior died, but his descendants are doctors as well, and they continue their quest for vampire blood. From what I was told, the vampires are afraid of the Hellinherrs."

"You want to sell the vampire?"

"For an enormous fee." She smiled. "And after we get the money from Cat, I want to pull her eyes out and then kill her slowly." Her hands curled to mimic claws.

"How much money will the doctor give us for a vampire?"

"The vampire's blood is priceless. My dad asked for half of the new enterprise."

"I like his thinking."

Chapter 27. Paying the Ransom

The phone rang and I jumped. "Hello?"

"Hello, Cat. How are you doing, girl?" Veronica asked in a cheery voice.

Better than you will, I thought. "What do you want?"

"We want to see you sooner."

"I haven't finished gathering all the information that I need for the money transfer."

"That's your problem. You stay by the phone at seven o'clock, and I'll call you and give you directions on how to come to us. By the way, don't bother wearing a wire or other shit like that. Goodbye."

They were accelerating the timetable. One reason might be to prevent me from making counterplans. Oh, I'd made counterplans already, as in transferring money to a Lichtenstein account that had a tracer virus to follow where the money ended up. I set up an alarm with my lawyers in case I went missing. I instructed Abe Yakowitz, my estate lawyer, not to transfer any of my properties unless I were there in person. I informed François about my plans and that I was wearing the tracking pendant he gave me. And, of course, I got my PI in the loop.

"Robert Mallon, PI agency. How may I help you?"

"Rob, this is Cat Sanders. I need you to follow me."

"Why? Are you in danger?"

"I might be, but before you worry too much, here is what I want you to do . . ." I told him my plan. "And one more thing—they may want me to enter the Silver Coffin through their subterranean access from the subway station. I'll probably be arriving at the station by the F line."

"OK, if I don't hear from you by tomorrow morning at 10 am, I'll call the police and report you kidnapped at the Silver Coffin," Rob confirmed.

"That's the plan. Wish me luck."

"Good luck!"

I was ready. My master plan was simple: Go there and go berserk.

At five o'clock the phone rang again. "Hello?"

"Cat, time to get moving." It was Veronica.

"You said seven."

"Oh, well, I lied. You have a half-hour to get to the Barnes & Noble on Fifth between 45th and 46th. If you don't do exactly what I'm telling you, Angelique gets the chainsaw."

She hung up. The first rendezvous was in a literary place. How prosaic! I had on my black sneakers, and black pants and shirt, and my hair was tied in a bun. I had money in my pockets and several hundred-dollar bills in my sneakers. I was ready.

Although Barnes & Noble wasn't far from where I lived, I took a cab and arrived there five minutes ahead of schedule. Wondering what their next move was, I walked around the bookshelves, trying to see if I could identify anyone or if I saw any

Goths. Everyone looked like a book lover. To stay busy, I checked a few books, and then I heard a phone ringing. Since I had no phone on me, I ignored it, but then something vibrated on my back. I reached around and found a cellphone clipped onto my belt. Someone, without me noticing, has planted it there.

"Hello?" I answered.

"Good. We can communicate now." Veronica sounded upbeat. "Go to 37th and Broadway, and wait for my call. You've got ten minutes."

I placed the phone in my pocket and scurried to the new location. Just before arriving there, the phone rang. "Do you see the tattoo parlor on 37th past Broadway? Go there."

I crossed Broadway and entered the tattoo shop. Posters of the most beautiful and bizarre designs plastered the walls. The high-pitched sound of a tattoo needle at work could be heard from behind a partition. A tall, mustachioed guy, appropriately tattooed and with a captain's hat on, came out to greet me. "Can I help you?"

"Someone sent me in here."

"For a tattoo?"

"I hope not."

"Who?"

"Veronica."

"Follow me." He took me to another room in the back and closed the door. "Lean against the wall and spread them out."

"What?"

"I need to frisk you. Make sure you don't have a wire or weapons on you."

"Crap." I placed my hands on the nearby wall and spread my legs.

He started with my hair bun. Then he moved his hands on my back down to the backs of my legs. I felt aroused, tickled, and ashamed. My face was burning. He moved his hands in front over my breasts and under my bra. He took his time, going down to my crotch and then in front of my legs.

"You're clean. Take your shoes off."

Double crap. I had money in my sneakers. I took them off and showed them to him.

"You always carry cash in your shoes?"

"Sometimes in my bra."

He grinned. "OK, put your shoes back on and let's go."

We went through another door, down some dilapidated corridors, and we exited on 36th.

"Go to Herald Square Station and take the F train going toward Brooklyn. I'll be following you to make sure you board the train. Go."

I walked two blocks south to the subway station with my tattoo buddy following me. At the station the phone rang.

"Take the F train and exit at 2nd Avenue and stay on the platform," Veronica said and then hung up.

My follower stood by me until I was on board. He even waved to me as the train departed the station. Rob the PI may not have kept up with me, but he knew I was going to be at the 2nd Avenue station, and so far I was right. All these precautions they took to get me to the place I suspected all along didn't look so brilliant. I didn't know if there was someone else from Veronica's gang following me now, but I was sure at the final destination someone would be waiting for me.

The subway stopped at the 2nd Avenue station, and the doors opened. I stepped out onto the platform and expected to see a marching band—not! A few minutes later the platform cleared and I was alone. A person in a black motorcycle outfit holding a spare helmet appeared out of nowhere. This was definitely her: my pursuer from a few nights ago.

She handed me the helmet. "Put it on."

I did as instructed, and, to my surprise, I couldn't see anything. The visor was opaque. In a fashion, I was blindfolded. She grasped me by the wrist and pulled me somewhere in the station. She had a strong grip. Next, I found myself yanked by my waist and placed at a lower level. Most likely she lowered me from the platform to the floor inside the tunnel. Dragging me by my wrist, she pulled me inside a damp place. We took many turns, and I was sure we ended in the drainage tunnels underneath the street. Eventually I heard a metal door banging open and I was pushed inside. The door was shut behind us and the woman ordered me, "Take off your helmet."

I gave the helmet back to her. We were inside a concrete corridor, lit by occasional fluorescent tubes on the ceiling.

"Walk," she told me. I did as she said, and she walked behind me until we reached another door, which she unlocked. Inside we took one flight of stairs up, stopping at a heavy wooden door, which she opened, and then she pushed me into a hall.

Chapter 28. The Throne Room

A large stone room surrounded me. Torches and candles provided all the illumination, giving the place a medieval ambiance. Red, velvety carpets covered the stone floor. Ahead of me I saw a throne, elevated five steps above the floor. The throne was located inside an alcove in the shape of a standing coffin. The man on the throne was in the shadow. Below the throne there were six Louis XVI gold and red velvet armchairs, three on each side. Melantha and Philomena, in black full court regalia, sat on either side of the throne. Veronica was seated, too, except she was dressed in white. Not a convert yet, I figured.

Those nut cases took that crap seriously—throne room, fake stone chamber, thick red carpet, flaming torches on the walls, courtiers, and me, summoned here. The biker returned and was dressed now in black Goth clothing. She sat on one of the other chairs. She had a shoulder holster with a revolver in it.

Did they want me to curtsy when I was in his royal presence? In their dreams.

"Come closer, Cat," the man invited me. I'd heard that voice before.

I moved closer—might as well let this charade begin.

To my surprise, Pink-Ass appeared from the shadows and brought an armchair for me, positioning it in front of the throne. His nose was red and blue, and his eyes had the beginnings of two shiners.

I walked to the chair and placed my hands on its high back, without sitting. "Where is Angelique?"

"What's your hurry?" Veronica asked, pleased to see me alone in their presence.

"Where is Angelique?" I shouted.

The man on the throne gestured, and from my left side I heard the creaking of pulleys and the clinking of chains. A platform resembling a ladder descended from the ceiling. To my horror, Angelique was on it. She was naked and covered in some kind of clear, thick plastic armor. That was how they'd bound her. The plastic encasement didn't cover her upper chest, neck, and head. Her legs were held together in shackles, and her hands were bound in chains over her head.

"What's the meaning of this?"

"This Angelique is a tough customer. We had to restrain her so she wouldn't hurt herself," said Philomena. "Or us."

"Pink-Ass, raised the rack vertically so we can see her better," said Melantha.

Pulling on the chains, Pink-Ass did as instructed, and Angelique was brought up to a near-vertical position. Her eyes were closed, and her head hung low.

I ran to her side to check on her. She seemed to be drugged. "Angelique, how do you feel? What did they do to you?" I raised her head and saw that she was alive. She opened her eyes slowly and focused on me. Then she closed them as slowly, but not before winking at me. Maybe she wasn't as drugged or wounded as they thought she was.

"Why is she like this? What did you give her?" I demanded.

"We gave her a dose of our elixir, the White Fog, to keep her subdued," said Philomena.

"Was that necessary?"

"And two bullets to knock her out cold." The biker woman spoke.

"You shot her? You bitch!" I screamed, and I could have killed her right then and there.

"Yes, and as you see, she's not dead. There are no exit holes and no bleeding. Curious, wouldn't you say?"

"Nisha, next time use silver bullets." Melantha started to laugh.

I pointed a finger at Nisha. "You're the one who followed me the other night."

She just smiled coldly.

"Why did you shoot the cabbie?"

"He didn't obey orders. Now he is in a better place, with 72 virgins and all that."

"Who are you, you there on the throne?" I pointed to the seated shadow.

"Ha, ha, ha. You don't recognize my voice?"

"Cadogan?"

"Prince Cadogan, to you," said Melantha pompously.

Prince Cadogan leaned out of the shadow, smiling at me with his black lips and cloudy blue eyes. His stainless steel horns sparkled.

"You were a soldier last time I met you. Who died and made you prince since then?"

"Watch your tongue, commoner!" shouted Melantha.

Cadogan was the Prince who operated from the shadows. And I thought he was a Goth gentleman. I returned to Angelique and placed my hand on her forehead. She was her usual, natural cold. I read her lips. She needed blood. One way or another, she would drink someone's blood, even mine, if needed.

"Well, Veronica, some nice company you keep," I remarked. "A step down, I'd say."

Veronica gave me the finger.

I crossed my arms and leaned on the rack Angelique was bound on.

"Prince Cadogan," demanded Melantha, pointing to me. "Who does she think she is? Make her pay for her transgression."

"A money payment will do just fine," said Cadogan. "Well, Veronica, she's all yours. Let's see if she'll pay up as promised."

"Of course she'll pay up. She's just grandstanding." Veronica got up and walked halfway toward Angelique and me.

"You remember our agreement," Philomena said silkily from behind. "If you get the money from her, you can keep half. But if we have to extract the money, you don't get a dime."

"Some agreement," I chuckled. "What makes you think that you'll get even a dime from these people? You gave the goods away. Consider yourself lucky if they let you live."

Veronica's demeanor changed from assured and in charge to doubtful and scared. "Well, I have more tricks up my sleeve. I have leverage. Like a certain Dr. Hellinherr."

Now it was my turn to feel unsure, and I probably went pale. I noticed Cadogan and Philomena exchanging knowing glances.

"How do you feel now?" She pointed to me. "Did you bring the account numbers?"

I glared at her. "Veronica, I'll pay you nothing. Not a cent."

She looked incredulous and furious. Philomena and Melantha snickered, as if they knew my answer.

"What did you say?" she ran toward me, enraged. "I'm a vampire slayer, and I'll kill her if you don't pay." From somewhere in her dress she pulled a silver dagger.

"Get behind me," whispered Angelique.

I obeyed.

"I'm going to kill this freak, if you don't do as I demand!" She thrust the dagger with all her might into Angelique's heart.

Chapter 29. Cat's Deal

I gasped in horror. I'd overplayed my hand. This couldn't be happening. Silver kills vampires.

Veronica raised a bent knife up in the air, perplexed over its shape and the lack of any blood flowing from Angelique.

Angelique opened her eyes and gave a deep throaty laugh. "A silver knife? Some vampire slayer."

"You forgot to give her the death kiss before killing her," I said to Veronica sarcastically.

Veronica screamed hysterically and lunged at Angelique to strangle her. I seized Veronica by the hair and pulled her head toward Angelique's mouth. Veronica screamed for a second and then she went limp, receiving a long, bloodsucking kiss from Angelique. At first no one realized that Angelique was drinking Veronica's blood. Veronica's hair covered the face of Angelique, whom she was supposedly kissing.

I sauntered toward the throne to let Angelique drink Veronica's blood unhindered. "OK, Cadogan, let's make a deal." They all looked at me expectantly.

A holler came from behind me. Pink-Ass pointed to Veronica. "Something's happening to Veronica!"

"Pull her off that freak!" shouted Cadogan.

Pink-Ass jumped into action, and pulling by her hair, he pried Veronica's head off Angelique. Veronica fell to the floor, unconscious. Pink-Ass kneeled quickly beside her, shaking her by the shoulders to revive her.

"What's the matter with her?" demanded Melantha, who ran toward them.

"I don't know." He lowered his ear to her heart. "She's alive. She's just fainted."

Melantha kneeled down and examined Veronica. She slapped Veronica several times until she opened her eyes. She was like a wet noodle, with hardly any strength left in her.

"Are you alright?" Melantha shouted at Veronica while shaking her.

"I'm fine," Veronica pushed her away and stood up. But she rose up too fast. Drained of blood, she fainted and collapsed back down to the floor.

Cadogan, followed by Nisha and Philomena, approached. It was no longer a formal, courtly event that was under their control. Things were going awry.

"What the hell is going on?" Cadogan was ticked off.

He asked me that question, but Melantha, who was trying to revive Veronica again, answered, "That freak did something to Veronica. I told you we should have killed her."

Veronica awoke again. This time she just sat up. "Cat, you'd better pay us what we asked you, or we will kill Angelique."

"Really?" I smirked. "With your silver knife—" I kicked the ridiculously bent knife away, "—or with your bare hands?"

"Cadogan, I have a feeling Cat is toying with us," said Philomena.

I crossed my arms. "If you want me to stop toying with you, you'd better take my deal."

"Your deal?" Veronica asked from the floor. "You're in no position to offer any deals."

Cadogan ignored her. "What deal do you have in mind, Cat?"

"Let me take Angelique out of here. And Veronica, too. Then I'll forget anything ever happened."

Cadogan laughed loudly, followed by Philomena and Melantha. "Are you mental?"

"Mental?"

"Crazy!" he shouted. "You and Angelique are my prisoners. Just because she has tough skin doesn't mean I cannot kill her. And you, little girl, you've got some nerve threatening me and promising no recourse for what I did. Your billions have gone to your head, making you think that you can boss anyone around," he said with a mocking sneer.

"If you only knew what I could do to you," I said coldly. I tried to hide my doubts that the Strigoi might not come to my aid. I was betting it all, either on a royal flush or a bluff.

"And what are you going to do to us, little girl?" jeered Cadogan.

Veronica, up on one knee, said, "You bitch, you'd better give us all your money, or you're going to be hamburger meat."

"Just like your father?" I answered. "He failed, and now his ashes are watching you from the sewer. I'm taking you to the FBI to tell them what you and your corrupt federal agent of a father did."

"Bitch!" she screamed. "You bitch, I'll kill you!"

"What federal agent? What FBI?" Cadogan was alarmed.

"Oh, I'm sorry." It was my turn to smirk. "She didn't tell you that the FBI and Homeland Security are looking for her?"

Cadogan looked at Veronica, infuriated. "You never told me about that aspect of your life."

"What difference does it make if my father was a federal agent? Why are we even discussing me? She's the one in trouble and I—me—I got her here." Veronica was defiant.

"Was the FBI and Homeland Security another ace in the hole, Veronica?"

Cadogan's face contorted with anger. He shook his finger at her, unable to tell her off.

"Veronica, thank you for telling us about the FBI's and Homeland Security's involvement in this," Philomena said calmly. "We contemplated giving you a slice of the pie for the information you brought to the table, but you're not worth anything. You made a big mistake, and you're not an asset anymore."

"What? What do you mean?" Veronica asked in a shaky voice.

"We don't need you anymore. We don't need any complications with the feds," said Philomena, pointing to her. "Nisha, pop her."

Veronica's face filled with fear and dread, as Nisha pulled out her gun and shot her between the eyes.

Chapter 30. Strigoi

These people were cold, black-souled murderers. Veronica was on her back with a hole between her eyes, a small trickle of blood running down her face. She had very little blood left in her, and only a small puddle formed behind her head. Strangely, I felt sorry for her.

"Thank you, Philomena and Nisha," Cadogan said placidly. "You got rid of a nuisance, a liar, and a rat who was involved with federal agents."

Drooling, Pink-Ass moved closer to see Veronica dead. His eyes were wild, as if he enjoyed seeing the dead woman. "Can I cut her with the chainsaw, Prince Cadogan?" He ran a thumb from his crotch to his head.

I felt my blood run cold. Without another thought, I pushed him toward Angelique, and she clenched him by the throat with her fangs. Pink-Ass screamed in agony, while squirming and pounding on Angelique. He was a dead man.

Nisha raised her gun and fired the remaining five shots from her revolver through Pink-Ass and Angelique. For sure, the .38-caliber bullets went through both of them. Pink-Ass lay motionless, leaning against Angelique, his blood gushing to the floor. She had her eyes closed while holding onto his throat. I was doubtful that Angelique was alive. Five bullets should have killed even a vampire.

"What the hell did you do that for?" Cadogan shouted. "I wanted her undamaged."

"Sorry, Prince Cadogan. I sensed the vampire was gaining strength with every drop of blood she sucked."

"Damn it!" Cadogan squared his shoulders. "Maybe she's not dead. But I don't have time for that now. Let's finish with her." He pointed to me and then snapped his fingers.

A cold reality descended on me. I was alone with them. They noticed my fear as it gripped me, and I swallowed hard. How foolish could I have been to go in there and attempt to rescue Angelique single-handedly?

While Nisha reloaded her revolver, Melantha and Philomena grabbed my arms and took me to my chair, where they pushed me down in it. Cadogan sat on his throne regally. Melantha and Philomena sat in their armchairs as if they were about to start a court session. On the floor in front of me, with her gun back in its holster, Nisha sat crossed-legged, holding a laptop as if she were the court transcriber.

"Let's get down to business, shall we?" said Cadogan from his high throne. "As you saw, we don't shy away from killing if we don't get what we want. And we want your billions. Give them to us. Now!" His eyes were cold and harsh, his horns were sharp, and his black lips framed his shouting mouth.

I stared at him, hoping that fear wouldn't overcome me completely. "Why would I do that?"

Dark figures entered the room. The watchers, Cadogan's army, dozens of them, came in and formed a circle, a black wall, around us. Angelique, with Pink-Ass still in her jaws, was left outside the circle. I recognized Spike, Goose, Lanky, Tiny, and more among them, all pale with black makeup around their eyes. They stared with empty eyes, emotionless, as if they were zombies. Maybe they were zombies, drugged, and no longer humans.

"If you want to live, that's why. Go ahead, Nisha."

"Let's start with one account at a time," demanded Nisha, with her fingers poised on the keyboard. "First account number?"

"No!" I shouted.

"Are you dense or something?" Melantha shouted back at me. "Do you want me to put you on the torture rack in place of your vampire friend?"

"If you think that I'm giving you a penny, or that you will get out of this scot-free or even alive, you're mistaken. And get these zombies out of here!" I motioned with my head to the circle of dark watchers. I was scared and I was pissed off.

Melantha came to me. "You bitch." She backslapped me.

I saw stars, and my right eye started tearing. One of her rings cut me and I felt the burning on my cheek, even though the right side of my face was numb from the slap. That was it. I stood up to lunge at her, but some of the watchers grabbed me and held me down, even by my hair. I struggled, but they had me pinned.

"Bring the insemination tool," ordered Cadogan.

Mohawk advanced toward me, holding a contraption like a mask in his hands, and tried to place it on my face. I screamed at the top of my lungs.

And suddenly I felt them. Screeching sounds, like nails running down a blackboard, flooded the throne room, and ephemeral shadows flew widely around us, among us, and in between us.

My Strigoi had come to my rescue and were ready for me to take action. I remembered what Vlad did when he used them. I opened my palms and raised my arms that several of the watchers were holding, but I felt no restraint. They were powerless and couldn't hold me down. My arms were up high, with my palms open, and a shock wave came from within me. I became the center of an explosion. Everyone who touched me and was near me was blown away. Some bounced off the ceiling, falling down in clumps, others flew up backward over the heads of the other watchers until they hit the hard walls. Screams of surprise, fear, and pain engulfed the chamber.

But that didn't stop the next row of watchers from attacking me. Fingers like talons reached toward me. Sneering and foaming from their mouths, with the eyes of rabid dogs, they advanced to tear me apart. I closed my hands into fists, wrapped my arms around me, and then I opened them wide. The explosion I commanded was even more powerful than before, leveling all the watchers. The lucky ones were entangled on the floor, trying to find their bearings. Many more died by bouncing off the ceiling or the walls. It was a mad house of screams and cries. The White Fog couldn't mask the pain they experienced from broken bones and torn bodies.

Melantha looked at me, eyes wide with fear. She seemed to be paralyzed by terror at what was happening around me, but then she gathered her wits and shouted, "Kill her!"

The surviving watchers collected themselves and got up from the floor, bleeding from all the metal piercings ripped from them during the shockwave I caused. Staggering, they ran toward me like a mob of screaming zombies, eyes fixed on me, teeth ready to tear off my flesh, arms stretched to rip me apart. They were oblivious to what had just happened to them. I raised my arms and spun, with my palms held open. As they approached me, each one hit an invisible wall with a thud. Blood erupted from their heads, faces, noses, and mouths, as they smashed into a solid, invisible shield. The sounds of broken bodies, bones, and skulls were deafening. They were thrown back, but new watchers attacked and hit the wall, and attacked again until there were no more standing up. Most, if not all, were surely dead or dying, corpses strewn on the floor with pools of blood around them. One of them hung from a wall torch, his clothes on fire.

Melantha, recovered from her panic and fear, her face contorted with hatred, was ready to attack me.

"Don't touch her!" shouted Philomena. "She possesses dark powers!"

Melantha stopped, trembling with anger, as she turned halfway toward Philomena.

"She has no power if we don't threaten or harm her," said Philomena, walking toward us.

"Let's see what she can do against a bullet," said Nisha, pointing her gun at me.

Chapter 31. Finishing the Job

I raised my hand and opened my palm. I hoped my Strigoi would protect me against a bullet, but they weren't around anymore. Doubt overcame me as I was about to be shot. How could I defend myself against a bullet? Even Angelique was killed by them. Nisha cocked the gun and pulled the trigger. I could see everything in slow motion. Just before the gun fired, a hand grabbed her forearm and lifted it. The gun fired, but the bullet went high and didn't touch me.

Angelique was there, alive, holding Nisha's arm high. She had her vampire face on: blue veins pulsing, eyes filled with blood, fangs shimmering with saliva, and ready to rip throats. Nisha dropped the gun and screamed in pain. Angelique twisted her arm and pulled it out of the socket. The most horrible scream escaped from Nisha's throat. Blood spurted out of her shoulder socket and she collapsed. Angelique jumped on her throat, breaking her neck like a pretzel.

"Well, ladies and Prince Spick-n-Span, it's payback time." Angelique sneered at them. "Time to die." She bared her one-inch long fangs.

She leaped at Melantha first, but the Goth grabbed Angelique by the throat. Big mistake. Angelique bit her hands off. Melantha stood there, watching her stubby forearms, blood squirting from them. She didn't get a chance to scream, because Angelique ripped her throat open. As she tried to breathe, her trachea gurgled from the blood flowing from her ripped throat, flooding her lungs and drowning her.

Philomena ran away. Angelique leaped across the hall and pounced on her. There was Philomena, flat on her face, dressed in her black gown, and a marble-white creature, Angelique, squatting on her like an animal of prey on top of her catch.

From the corner of my eye, I saw Cadogan's coffin-throne spin around, and he disappeared behind a wall that replaced his throne. The bastard had escaped!

I turned to Angelique and said, "Don't kill her."

She looked at me, blood dripping from her fangs.

"Please, don't kill me!" Philomena pleaded, scared out of her mind. "I'm not a vampire slayer like Veronica. I love vampires. I want to be one just like you. Make me a vampire, please!"

"Cadogan's escaped," I said. "And I need to know where Veronica's files are." I wiped the sweat from my brow. Then I touched my cheek. It felt raw and it hurt.

"This is your lucky hour," Angelique told Philomena as she pulled her up like a ragdoll from the back of the neck. "You'd better show us where the files are."

"And you'll let me go?"

"If you make it worthwhile for me, I'll think about it."

"Where did Cadogan escape to?" I asked Philomena.

"Cadogan?" She looked around, disoriented. She didn't know he had escaped. "There are many escape routes. I don't know."

I went up the steps to where the throne once was. "How about here?" I knocked on the fake wall. It was made of steel.

"I didn't know that was there." Philomena was so scared that she couldn't even conceive of lying.

Angelique stripped one of the watchers and put on some clothes. She came next to me and forced open partially the steel wall. I squeezed inside. It was dark, but I could see a stairway leading up somewhere. Cadogan was gone.

I pulled myself back. "I think the files are more important." I turned to see Angelique, but she was dragging Philomena by one leg back into the throne room. She had attempted to escape. Angelique flung her across the floor toward me.

"Please don't kill me!" pleaded Philomena on her knees, with her hands raised to protect herself.

"Get up and take us to retrieve Veronica's files," Angelique commanded.

On our way out, next to the broken torture rack where once Angelique was pinned down, I noticed the acrylic encasing armor lying in shards on the floor. "How did you manage to break that?"

"The bullets Nisha used were hollow points. They went through Pink-Ass and cracked the acrylic plates. After that, it was just a matter of breaking my way out of them and out of the shackles."

Philomena took us upstairs, where the apartments were located, all the way to Cadogan's apartment and office in the penthouse. Behind his desk, Philomena opened the hinged painting of—

169

guess who? a portrait of a fake Dracula—and showed us the safe. "I don't know the combination."

Angelique snatched her by the throat and shoved her through a nearby window. The glass and the window frame broke and fell down below into the street. Both Angelique and Philomena were balancing on the windowsill, Angelique holding Philomena by the throat. "My patience is wearing thin. What is the combination?"

"I really don't know," Philomena managed to say while her eyes bulged out.

"So be it." Angelique released her throat.

Philomena flapped her arms to regain her balance and prevent her fall. "Please, I don't know," she begged.

"Maybe for once you're being honest." Angelique reached out and grabbed her by the hair to pull her back in. But Philomena's long black hair was a wig, and she fell backward, landing ten stories down on the sidewalk. Her scream ended with a thump. "Oops, I didn't know," said Angelique, holding the wig, which she then threw out the window.

"How are we going to open the safe?"

"Don't worry, hon. I can open it, but it will take a minute." She placed her ear close to the safe. "By the way, we need to burn this place down."

"But there may be people alive in the throne chamber."

"And if they are? Cadogan was a chemist and developed an engineered drug that enslaved those watchers. Those people were his zombies. Go to the first floor of the apartments, and you'll find a door with 'Dispensary' written on it. Kick the door down, get in, and you'll find a lot of those drugs there. They are flammable. Near the desk there is a hatch. Open it and throw all the jars with the drugs down that shaft. I'll meet you in the throne room." She turned to the safe and carefully began rotating the dial, with her ear flat against the vault door.

I didn't argue. There was no good way out of this. I ran down the stairs to the floor where I found the Dispensary and, to my surprise, the door was unlocked. I entered and found the hatch on the floor, opened it, and threw all the jars with the white stuff down the shaft as instructed.

After my task was complete, I returned to the throne room where I found Angelique piling up the bodies and getting ready to start a pyre. She dispensed the drugs from a plastic bucket onto the bodies. The stuff resembled sour cream, although it smelled like something flammable.

"There you are," Angelique said. "I hope this stuff will not ignite by itself before we leave. Do you know how Nisha brought you here?"

"No, she blindfolded me. But wait, I'm sure they have an exit to the underground garage from here. I'll be right back." I ran to where Cadogan had disappeared behind his throne and took the stairs up. As expected, I found a steel door that opened into the underground garage. That was where Cadogan escaped to, and he probably had a car for a quick getaway.

I returned to the throne room. Angelique was finished, admiring her pile of bloody corpses smeared with White Fog.

Oh my God! We were about to commit mass murder. What was I saying? I committed mass murder when I flung dozens of watchers into the ceiling and the walls. Vlad had warned me that when you're rich, the stakes are much higher and you must do atrocious things. I thought I'd have to deal with unscrupulous lawyers, greedy financiers and bankers, Wall Street shysters, corrupt politicians, devious conmen, and depraved socialites. I didn't expect this—mass murdering drugged-out-of-their-minds people. But then, were they people or were they zombies?

"What about the nightclub? There could be people in there." I voiced my concern to Angelique.

"The nightclub doesn't open until later. The club will burn, too, but only from the flames coming from here and the Vampire's Lair. The fire alarm will scare the remaining people out."

That sounded as good as it was going to be. "I found the exit," I told Angelique.

"Very good, hon. Go back behind the throne." She lit a bunch of rags from a torch and dropped it onto the pyre. It started burning slowly, but soon it engulfed the whole pile. Fingers of fire spread out along the white drug paths Angelique had laid on the floor and the carpets, connecting to the rest of the club. "Let's get the hell out of here!"

She ran my way and together we exited into the garage. "We need to split up, and we will meet later at the safe house. Here is the DVD with the

172

information Veronica had. One more thing—I don't have any money."

I took off one of my sneakers and gave her all the bills I had in it. We embraced and headed in different directions, holding our heads down. Philomena's body had not been discovered yet. The fire alarms have not been triggered. So far it was all quiet this evening around the building. But not for long.

Chapter 32. What They Wanted

I took a long, hot shower. I was exhausted and needed the cleansing. The previous Cat, the one who had existed before experiencing François the vampire killing my kidnappers, would have been catatonic by now. Now I just felt sad.

I looked in the mirror; my right eye was darkening. I was going to have a black eye. My first. I applied medication and a bandage to my scratched cheek. Luckily, it wasn't that bad.

Dressed in my robe and with a towel around my wet hair, I reviewed the messages on my phone. Rob Mallon had left several; in the last one, he sounded desperate. I put a raw steak on my eye, turned the TV on, and called Rob back.

"Hi, Rob."

"Cat, is that you? Thank God! The Silver Coffin's building is on fire."

On TV, they showed a massive fire burning the back portion of the building. The FDNY was deployed in force, trying to save at least the front of the building and to prevent the closest building on the back street from catching fire. Jets of water from the fire hoses gushed through the blown-out windows, trying to squelch the inferno. Discreetly, of course, I was going to make good for whatever the insurance wouldn't pay for the damage to that building.

"I'm alright, Rob. Don't worry."

"I'm so sorry I lost you at the 2nd Avenue station when that biker took you down the tracks. I went after you, but it was as if the tunnel had swallowed you up."

"I was blindfolded with an opaque helmet, Rob. I don't know where I was taken. But I managed to escape and now I see that the building is burning down."

"What happened?"

"Let's say I was lucky to escape alive. Please don't mention this to anyone. I'm counting on your silence."

"You have my word."

"Now I have a new job for you."

"You do? You won't fire me for not protecting you?"

"Why should I fire you? Relax. I want you to find Cadogan, the Goth, although he may have found a new religion by now."

"Cadogan the Goth. Got it. I took his picture several times."

"Yep, that's him. He was running a drug lab in there. That may be the cause of the fire. But that's confidential. Let the police and the fire department unravel the mystery."

"Understood."

I deactivated all the emergency missing-person warnings, including the one sent to Abe Yakowitz. I left a message for François; in case he hasn't already departed, he could cancel his trip if he wished. I was safe. Outside the window, it was night, and there weren't going to be any more watchers.

Angelique came over. Holding a tall drink as usual, she looked refreshed but tired. I had a glass of wine, because I needed it for sure. We didn't talk; we just enjoyed each other's quiet company.

Angelique broke the silence. "This has been a hell of a year," she sighed.

"You don't say." I patted her hand. "How did you get caught?"

She told me the story of how she penetrated the inner rooms of the Silver Coffin and how she was trapped in the epoxy cement. "I didn't think that they were aware of my presence, but they were, and they got me in a perfect trap that no vampire could escape."

"You could have suffocated."

"Sure, but I kept my head above the muck line."

"How did they extract you from the hard epoxy?"

"They cut it open with a diamond blade. I was pulled out of it like a doll out of a mold."

"But weren't you able to fight them once you were out of it?"

"Oh, yes. Before they cut me out of it, the Prince and Philomena convinced me to swallow the White Fog. That stuff affected me from the time I first drank the blood of the watchers. After taking the White Fog, it made me sluggish. They attached a steel collar around my neck and shackles connected by a heavy chain, and that's how they handled me. At one point, when I was uncontrollable, Nisha shot me twice. The entry holes sealed quickly without bleeding, but the bullets are inside me."

"Oh, God!"

"I'm a vampire. I was shot once before. As long as I'm not shot in the heart or decapitated, I'll be OK."

"How did you manage to hold the samurai blade with your hand and get shot, and not bleed?"

"Long ago, after the first time I was shot, I asked François about why I didn't bleed. He's a doctor, and he knows this stuff. We vampires have blue blood—it is based on copper, and that's why it's blue—unlike your blood, which is red because it is based on iron. Also, our blood is thicker, more viscous, and doesn't flow as easily as red blood. But that's not the reason I don't bleed. Vampire blood and its blue blood cells carry antibodies and coagulants so that, when a cut happens, they attack any microbes present and immediately seal the skin. Nisha's blade cut my palm, but it sealed immediately, and the wound created by the cut became a hard scab that resisted deeper penetration by the blade. The same thing happened with the bullets after they penetrated my skin—the holes closed instantly. The bullets were hollow points, and they broke inside my body and did not exit."

"But what happened to your internal organs? Didn't they get damaged?"

"Sure, but my organs are recovering. We heal fast. That's why I need human blood. It helps the healing and the rejuvenation of our vampire cells. Human blood is our life energy."

"Hmm. Blue blood." I touched the bump behind my right ear, where the blue blood ampule was inserted.

"François thinks that we vampires have more in common with the horseshoe crab than with humans. The horseshoe crab has blue blood as well, and they bleed to death only if they are pierced through the heart. That's why we can be killed only if we're stabbed through the heart or our heads are severed. No brain to control the body, no life."

"That's why the legend says to drive a stake through a vampire's heart or cut his head off to kill him."

"It could be, but a wooden stake will not penetrate the skin. It would have to be steel, with a lot of force applied to it."

"You're indestructible."

"I wouldn't say that. We can be blown to pieces by a bomb. We need oxygen just like you do, although we can hold our breaths for a longer time than you can."

"When you were entrapped in epoxy, Nisha could have cut your head off with the circular saw."

Angelique nodded. "That was my biggest fear. But they were interested in the whole of me. Yes, they were aspiring vampire slayers, but first they wanted to be just like me—vampires."

"Catching you was a bonus."

"They expected your great-grandfather, Vlad, to come after them and somehow capture him. Veronica was working on the extortion angle, Cadogan was after the vampire stuff, and that was, in a nutshell, what they tried to do."

"Vampire blood and billions," I said philosophically. "You looked awful when I saw you on that torture rack."

"I'm glad you understood that I needed blood to heal and to counteract the White Fog. I gained energy when the fools gave me pure alcohol to weaken me. Luckily, Veronica's blood wasn't contaminated with the drug, which was good, and it was just what I needed. I didn't drink Pink-Ass's blood because he was drugged." After a pause, Angelique looked seriously at me. "I didn't know you had those powers."

"They are Strigoi. I inherited them from Vlad. They come to my rescue when there is an imminent threat or I'm in pain."

Angelique smiled at me. She was happy that I was not totally defenseless.

"We had a close call." I shuddered and took a drink of my wine.

"Like I said, a hell of a year. I'm glad you're with me, in case I need rescuing again."

We both laughed. Me, a mere mortal, rescuing a vampire? That was a hoot.

"We got rid of Veronica, or they got rid of her, but now we have Cadogan on the loose. I wonder if he knows about Hellinherr." I was concerned.

"If he does, I'm sure he'll contact him. What's François doing?"

"He's coming to New York."

The next day I called Rob Mallon. "Hi Rob, any news on Cadogan?"

"Not yet, Cat. I hired a young PI who makes a good Goth, and he's checking other Goth clubs and inquiring about him."

"OK, but Cadogan was not a true Goth. He was just using those people. By now, he might be a clean-cut, respectable gentleman of society. Oh, yes, he used to be a chemist. Judging by his age, mid-thirties, he graduated around the end of the millennium."

"Thanks for that clue. I'll check on the graduates around that time from the schools around here, and then expand from there."

"And also I want you to find a Dr. Hellinherr. He may be in Virginia. There is an organization called the Hellinherr Institute of Health and Longevity. Follow and document his whereabouts discreetly."

"No problem."

"Rob, I'll be out of the country for a week or so. Just set up a dossier on Hellinherr."

"I'll do that, and have a good trip."

"Thanks!"

I disconnected and hoped for a good trip to Transylvania. And François was arriving that evening. I could barely wait to look into his Caribbean-blue eyes.

The End

Other Books by Mit Sandru

Thank you for reading my book. If you enjoyed it and would like to help other readers with your comments please write a review on Amazon. And of course I much appreciate your review as well. **Amazon book** link.

For more information about my books please visit **sandru.com**

Or visit me at my website: sandru.com and subscribe to my mailing list.

(your e-mail will not be sold or used for spam)

Vampire Thriller & Romance

Vampire (Vlad V Series), by Mit Sandru, a Vampire Romance.

Vampire (Vlad V, Book 1) by Mit Sandru.

Meeting a vampire isn't something that happens every night, even on the New York City subways. Even in her wildest dreams Cat never expected to meet a vampire or survive an encounter with one. Instead, she becomes his confidant. Why is she so lucky?

R.I.P., The Death of a Vampire (Vlad V, Book 2) by Mit Sandru.

The US intelligence agencies have a massive database, including pictures that can identify any person in the US and abroad. A search has found a photograph of Vlad V Draculesti, a man living in present-day Manhattan, dating from 1851. How can that be? Why does Vlad look the same in the 21st century as he did in the 19th? Who is this man who has lived such a long life?

Homeland Security Federal Agent John Miller discovers that Vlad V Draculesti is a vampire, and he blackmails Vlad for billions of dollars, threatening to divulge that information to the authorities or to the evil Dr. Hellinherr, who is trying to create a super-race of people through the use of vampire blood.

But Vlad V, because of a mishap, is now dying of old age, and all he wants is to die in peace. Cat Sanders, his great-granddaughter, and his three vampire friends—François, Angelique, and Mundibuto—come to his rescue. They foil the intelligence agencies' plans to discover the real identity of Vlad V Draculesti, and they eliminate the corrupt federal agent's threat. Never underestimate a vampire, his cunning great-granddaughter and his vampire friends.

Vampire Slayers (Vlad V, Book 3) by Mit Sandru.
Vlad V the vampire warned Cat that when you're rich,
the stakes are much higher, and that she might have to
do appalling things to survive. Cat thought she'd have to
deal with unscrupulous lawyers, greedy financiers and
bankers, Wall Street shysters, corrupt politicians,
devious conmen, and depraved socialites. Instead, an old
nemesis allied with a vampire-slayer drug cult came out
of the dark, demanding extortion money or she would be
killed. Capturing a vampire—Vlad V perhaps—would be
an added bonus for the cult. Blue vampire blood could
provide perpetual life and additional riches.
Unfortunately, the villains don't know who or what they
are dealing with. Never upset the great-granddaughter
of Vlad V and Angelique, her vampire friend, if you want
to stay healthy and alive.

Vampires of Transylvania (Vlad V, Book 4)

Cat has a simple task ahead of her: spread Vlad V Draculesti's ashes in Transylvania at midnight during a full moon. But it won't be that simple. She comes across Vlad V and Vlad the Impaler's old enemies and a sinister plot concocted by the Queen of Vampires. By discovering the queen's plot, Cat finds herself in mortal danger.

Luckily, the African vampire Mundibuto and a new friend, Dr. Tudor Lupu, come to her aid. She has to use all the tricks she can muster to stay alive and take revenge on Vlad the Impaler's assassins.

Soon to be published:
The Queen of Vampires (Vlad V Book 5), by Mit Sandru

Other Books:

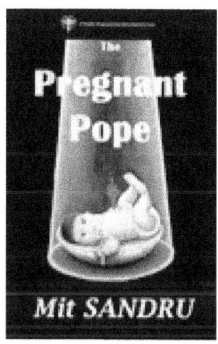

The Pregnant Pope (TIO Series), by Mit Sandru.

In the year of Satan, 2066, the structure of the physical world is cracking, and inexplicable paranormal forces are interfering with humanity. The Trinity Investigation Organization, or TIO—a paranormal detective society— is the last protection against the demons, evil spirits, fanatical criminals, and sadists who are trying to destroy the world.

The 92-year-old Pope is pregnant. Although he hasn't undergone any medical procedures, he carries a human fetus in his abdomen. Is this a case of self-cloning, or is it a mutation? Is this an immaculate conception, or is it Satan's work?

Claire, Travis, and Prescott, the members of the Capuchin Trinity Team of TIO, are tasked with uncovering the truth about this unusual case and resolving the mystery of whether the Pope is carrying the new Messiah or the Antichrist, and who did it. Their job is to go beyond the physical world into the mind and the spiritual realm, discover a thousand-year-old connection, perform an exorcism, and fight the devil Zepar, while evading the villains who keep trying to assassinate them.

Folding Reality, by Mit Sandru, a Paranormal, Time Travel Adventure.

Experiencing a new reality is just a paper-fold away for Mike the insurance salesman. But those realities are not by his choice and he ends up being crucified, or gassed at Auschwitz, or marooned in space in a Russian capsule.

Arboregal, the Lorn Tree, by D.G. Sandru, a Teen Fantasy and Science Fiction adventure.

Four young Americans are magically transported to a world where monsters roam the land, magnificent trees support all life, and an evil spirit hunts one of them to fulfill a deadly prophecy.

Escape from Communism, by Dumitru Sandru, a True Story and Commentary.

Life under communism is cruel and inhumane. Communist countries have a "Berlin Wall" around them, and the whole country is a giant concentration camp. I risked my life to escape from hell and reach freedom.

T-Shirts and other stuff:

Sandru's Shop or Sandru's Products

Visit my e-Gallery at:

http://dumitru-sandru.artistwebsites.com/
http://www.artistrising.com/galleries/Sandru

About Dumitru "Mit" Sandru

Dumitru "D.G." "Mit" Sandru was born in the greater area of Transylvania in the last century. He is an artist, composer, and author. He paints in the classical, surreal, and modern styles, and most of the music Dumitru composes is of the New Age flavor. As an author, he prefers to write Science-Fiction, Paranormal, and Teen/Children Fantasy & Sci-Fi novels.

Dumitru resides in California with his wife. They have one daughter and two grandsons.

Visit him at sandru.com